PAYBACK

ALSO BY VANESSA KIER

<u>The Surgical Strike Unit (SSU) Series</u>

Vengeance

Betrayal

Retribution

Payback

Aftermath

Undercover (Prequel Novella)

<u>The WAR Series</u>

WAR: Disruption

WAR: Intrusion

WAR: Opposition

PAYBACK

THE SURGICAL STRIKE UNIT
BOOK FOUR

VANESSA KIER

CHAPTER ONE

"I'M SORRY, FAITH."

Faith Andrews raised her shoulder in order to pin her cell phone closer to her ear and tightened her grip on her grocery bags. She'd broken another Bluetooth headset, dammit, and hadn't gotten around to replacing it yet.

"I haven't found any reference to Toby during my investigation," Siobahn Murphy added.

Faith grimaced as she climbed the front steps to her house. She'd really hoped her friend and former colleague would have good news for her. Siobahn's skills as an investigative journalist were legendary. Her ability to ferret out information no one wanted to reveal was nothing short of spooky. Because of the article Siobahn had written about missing military and law enforcement personnel, Faith had contacted her friend and asked for help locating her brother. Toby, an officer with military intelligence, had been missing for a month. "Thanks, anyway, Siobahn."

"Are you going to tell me what's really going on?"

"I don't know much more than we've already discussed." Faith used her body to trap the grocery bags against the door as she fumbled for her house keys in her purse. "Toby was on a long-term, ultra secret assignment. Before he left, he promised to check in at least every two weeks via our secure email account."

The grocery bags slipped and threatened to break free of her one-handed grip. Where were her blasted keys? "But he missed his last two check-ins. I've called all his friends and coworkers that I had contact info for and no one has seen or heard from him. I'm worried."

Worried was putting it mildly. Despite his job often taking him away for long periods of time, Toby never failed to check in. He knew how paranoid Faith was about losing him—her best friend and last living family member.

The grocery bags slipped another few inches toward the ground, forcing Faith to bend her knees and shove her hips closer to the door to prevent the bags from falling to the wet porch. She shoved her free hand deeper into her purse and her fingers touched cool metal. "Ah! Finally."

"Faith?" Siobahn's voice held a hint of amused exasperation. Something Faith had heard all too often during the years they'd worked together. Siobahn expected to receive your full attention and didn't appreciate knowing you were multi-tasking while talking to her.

"Sorry. I'm trying to get the groceries inside and finally found my keys."

Siobahn sighed. "I don't see how small town life can possibly suit you. Let someone else teach those snarky high schoolers and over privileged college students about journalism and come back to work for me." Siobahn was a senior investigative reporter with one of the most prominent national newspapers. She headed a team of journalists known for their in-depth, hard-hitting reporting and Faith had once been proud to call herself a member of the team. But that life of constantly chasing down the truth to the exclusion of all else no longer appealed to her.

"You know you're missing the adrenaline rush of investigating a hot story," Siobahn cajoled.

"Actually, you'd be surprised at how much trouble a group of hormonal teenagers can cause. I get plenty of excitement." Faith yanked the keys out of her purse, shoved the house key into the lock, and snatched her grocery bags with both hands as the door swung open.

Unfortunately, her action caused her shoulder to lower. The phone dropped, landing on top of the stack of mail on the hardwood floor. Faith settled the grocery bags out of the way as she picked up her phone.

"Faith? Are you okay?"

"Ugh. Yes. Just dropped the phone. Listen, I—"

"No Faith, you listen. You're one of the best journalists I've ever trained. You're wasting your talent with that high school newspaper and those Intro to Journalism classes you're teaching at the college. You need to stop punishing yourself for what happened and get on with your life."

Faith sucked in a breath, the pain still sharp even after more than a year. Trust Siobahn to be the one person who confronted her head-on about her decision to quit journalism.

"I really appreciate your support, Siobahn. You're a good friend. But..." Faith closed the front door and dumped her keys back in her purse, then bent down to pick up her mail. A large manila envelope sticking out from the bottom of the stack caught her attention. Curious, she turned it over.

The return address was for an unfamiliar lawyer's office, but Faith's address was written in Toby's precise handwriting. She froze. The room spun and she closed her eyes until the dizziness passed.

Toby, who'd been missing for a month, had sent her a package from New York City two days ago?

"I've got to go, Siobahn. Thanks again for trying to find Toby," she said woodenly. She eyed the envelope warily. What if something terrible had happened to her brother? What if this envelope contained Toby's last will and testament?

Ignoring Siobahn's protest, Faith thumbed off the phone and tossed it onto the small table containing her landline phone. Then she walked to her office at the back of the house, set the envelope on her desk and just stood there with the letter opener in her hand. Unable to act. Unable to face the possibility that her brother might really be gone.

Just open it. Since when have you become such a coward?

She shook her head over the familiar argument. She'd become a coward the day eighteen months ago when her sister Lyndi had shot their parents to death, then turned the gun on herself.

But if Faith's years as an overseas investigative journalist had taught her anything, it was that delaying bad news didn't lessen the impact.

She took a deep breath and quickly slit open the end of the envelope. A stack of papers slid out, followed by two flash drives and a note written in Toby's precise script on a piece of lined notebook paper.

Faith,

If you're reading this note, then I've either been captured or killed and you need to go into hiding immediately. Grab everything essential, then follow our emergency plan.

Love, Toby

Faith stared in horror at the scrawled note. Toby had always joked that if the shit hit the fan and he ended up involved in an investigation that pitted him against his own superiors, he'd have to go on the run. The assumption had always been that anyone looking for Toby would immediately focus on Faith, so he'd made her practice evasive tactics as well. Their emergency plan involved a series of steps intended to help her disappear off the grid.

The familiar rush of adrenaline kicked in. Within ten minutes, Faith had gathered everything she needed and had slipped out the back door.

Two days later, Faith sipped her third cup of coffee and stared blearily at the Atlantic shoreline through the kitchen window of Toby's safe house. After walking out of her neighborhood by cutting through backyards, she'd taken a circuitous route to collect some of the items Toby had hidden. She now had a nondescript dark gray sedan registered under a false name, Toby's backup pistol, and this remote cabin on the coast to serve as her temporary home. The place was as off-the-grid as Toby could make it. A generator provided electricity and a well supplied water. There was no Internet connection and the stove ran on propane.

She'd removed her SIM card from her cell phone, then flushed the card down a public toilet and tossed the phone into a dumpster. Even though she had no sense of being followed, she'd still tossed and turned these past two nights, startling at every little creak and groan of the house.

Behind her, spread out on the kitchen table, were Toby's printed notes and Faith's own handwritten comments. "Toby, you idiot," she murmured. Not because she was mad at him for carrying on an investigation that had apparently resulted in his disappearance. But because he'd had the gall to tell Faith not to try and find him.

Most likely I'm dead, Toby had written in his second note, which he'd clipped inside the cover of his printed report. *I hope I'm dead and not captured. You'll understand why after reading my report.*

Remember how I told you I was investigating something

extremely sensitive? This is it. But I wasn't assigned to this investigation. In fact, my superiors think I'm on extended leave. What I stumbled upon is so dangerous, I don't know who to trust.

Except for you.

I want you to make this information public, Faith. I know you still have contacts at the top newspapers in the country. I know you'll find a way to take this information and form it into an exposé. But only pass it on to a person you trust implicitly not to reveal my findings ahead of time to anyone in the government. If word gets back to the people involved, your life and the life of any journalist who helps you will be at risk.

If there's no one you trust with your life, then leave the story alone.

Right. Like you'd ever do that.

But please, don't investigate my disappearance. I'm serious, Faith. Let me go.

I love you and I know this will be the hardest thing in the world for you, but please don't search for me. After the program has been exposed and taken apart, then maybe you'll be able to discover what happened to me. But don't try to find me before that. If I'm not dead, then they'll have turned me into a creature that won't recognize you and will kill on their order.

There are dozens of men whose lives depend on you taking down the program. They'll soon be beyond the point of saving if you don't act swiftly to blow this whole thing open.

Please. You have to save the victims. My death will be worth it if I know that no more men will suffer. The world needs to know that good, honorable men are being turned into conscienceless monsters by their own government. That the people whose job it is to protect these men instead look the other way and pretend nothing untoward has happened.

I'm counting on you, little sister.

Peace and love be with you.

Toby.

Faith had read Toby's note again and again until she couldn't make sense of the words through her tears. Even now, hours after she'd first read the note, indignation and fury warred with fear. How dare Toby ask her to make such a promise? How could he possibly think that she wouldn't do everything in her power to find him if there was a chance he was still alive?

Her throat tightened and she closed her eyes, pressing the rim of her coffee cup against her lips. In typical Toby fashion, he'd decided on the right thing to do and expected Faith to fall into line. She shook her head. His personality had always seemed better suited toward commanding men rather than spying on them. But her brother had claimed he loved the challenge of rooting out information and trying to make strategic sense out of it.

She sighed and opened her eyes, watching as dawn painted the horizon with pastel shades of pink and blue. Toby might have been one of the youngest military intelligence officers to gain his rank, and he might have a razor sharp mind when it came to analyzing data, but he was an idiot when it came to understanding the human heart.

The proof lay in the fact that he'd told Faith not to search for him. Clearly Toby had learned nothing from her reaction to the deaths of their parents and Lyndi. For God's sake, she'd quit her travel intensive job in order to make a home close to their grandmother, their only surviving relative. That should have given Toby a clue that Faith's priorities now lay entirely with her family. Even when Gramma had died two months later, Faith hadn't returned to being an overseas investigative journalist. Instead, she'd picked up and moved to Maryland so she could be closer to Toby.

But apparently her brother still thought Faith was the same driven woman who'd chased stories across the world rather than stay home and deal with the hero worship from her difficult sister. Well, Toby would learn differently when she located him and pulled his ass out of whatever trouble he'd gotten himself into.

First, though, she'd have to find out where he was.

After taking a final swig of coffee, Faith set another pot to brew then settled at the kitchen table. Toby had apparently been investigating the same mysterious disappearances of military and law enforcement personnel as Siobahn. While Faith waited for the coffee to finish brewing, she started combing through first Siobahn's article, then Toby's report, and finally his files on the two flash drives, searching for clues that would lead her to her brother.

What emerged was a chilling picture. A network that targeted men within the law enforcement and military communities, arranged for their kidnappings, then sent the men to a lab where they underwent treatment intended to turn them into superhuman soldiers. In the meantime, the victims were reported as dead.

Faith shivered and rubbed her arms. Unfortunately, while Toby had uncovered the existence of the program, he did not know who was in charge on the scientific end. He also hadn't learned what, exactly, was being done to the men. Only that several of the missing men had shown up hundreds of miles from where they'd last been spotted. They'd been bulked up on what appeared to be steroids, and had suffered from insane rage.

Faith was beginning to understand why Toby would rather be dead than be captured. Still, she had to cling to the hope that he was alive and she could find him. But to do that, she needed help. She didn't have the contacts within the military and law enforcement communities necessary to investigate the program. Because she was Toby's sister, his friends and colleagues had already spoken to her about his disappearance. Yet even getting them to admit to her that they hadn't seen Toby in a while had been as painful as pulling teeth. Faith didn't think they'd be any more forthcoming if she started asking pointed questions.

But Siobahn's father and brothers were all either in the military or law enforcement. Much as she hated to involve her friend, Faith needed help.

"Faith, my God, are you okay?" Siobahn demanded when Faith called her that evening from a disposable cell phone.

"What?" Faith halted at the base of a sand dune and stared at the water of Chesapeake Bay. This beach down from Baltimore offered the advantage of both privacy and the relative safety of a few dozen tourists who strolled at the edge of the water or huddled in groups to watch the sunset. Plus, it had multiple escape routes. "Yes. Of course. I'm fine. What's wrong?"

"What's wrong is that someone has been poking around the newspaper, asking about you."

"About me?" Faith slapped down the hem of her yellow-and-orange flower print sundress, hoping she appeared to be just another tourist unwilling to unplug from her electronics.

"Yes. When did we last see you? Talk to you? Were you working on any freelance projects for the paper, etc. Sheesh, girl, what kind of trouble are you in?"

Faith squeezed her eyes shut. So. The hunt was on. She'd have to assume that meant Toby had given up information about his safe house. As soon as she finished her call with Siobahn, she'd have to find a new place to stay. Thank goodness she'd been paranoid enough this afternoon to pack up all of her things and put them in the car, just in case. "Who was asking? Anyone official?"

"Yes. Well, sort of." Siobahn gave a skeptical snort. "You'd think the Department of Defense would realize that an experienced reporter can sense a lie. The story is that your brother went AWOL a few days ago and they want to talk to you as part of their investigation. But they've been unable to find you. However, I remembered that you said it had been almost a month since you heard from Toby, so I figured my visitor was up to no good. Therefore, I repeat, what trouble have you gotten yourself into?"

"Not me," Faith corrected. "Toby. Before he disappeared, he took official leave in order to continue his personal investigation into the missing military and law enforcement personnel."

"Well, crap."

"Yeah. Apparently an army friend of his went missing and was later reported dead. Some time later, Toby saw a glimpse of him on the news. When he started looking into it, Toby discovered evidence that made him think people he worked with might be involved. So he asked for time off and went into hiding." Which scared Faith to death, because if Toby had been captured while in hiding, what chance did she, whose clandestine skills were meager compared to her brother's, have of surviving? "Whoever is responsible for the disappearances likely kidnapped Toby, so you need to be careful, too."

"Which is why you left me a voicemail with the code that meant we had to use disposable phones for this conversation."

"Yes." Faith took a deep breath. "But that's not the main reason I called you. Siobahn, in your research into the missing service personnel did you ever come across reference to Kerberos?"

"Kerberos?" Siobahn replied. "Yeah, that rings a bell. Hold on."

Faith scanned her surroundings for danger signs while she waited for Siobahn to pick up the phone again. She'd decided not to call Siobahn from Toby's cabin, even though she was using a disposable cell phone. She didn't know if technology existed that could somehow tap into their phone call and trace it back to a location, but figured it was best to err on the side of extreme caution.

With Siobahn's news, however, Faith feared for both her own safety and Siobahn's. Although her friend's article had been published a few weeks ago, she suspected that Toby's disappearance indicated a decision to eliminate all possible sources of information on Kerberos. Which could lead them to decide to kill Siobahn, just in case she knew more than she'd printed.

Not that Siobahn's article had gone into great detail. It merely suggested that the missing personnel had been kidnapped, and implied that people in several branches of the government had been involved in faking the men's deaths and funneling them into the superhuman soldier program. However, Siobahn hadn't pointed the finger at any one particular organization being in charge. Or given details about the scientific program.

On the other hand, when Faith had finally cracked the encryption on Toby's second flash drive, she'd found documents linking the scientific program to a group called Kerberos, run out of the CIA. Toby believed people within the DOD and the law enforcement community had been working with Kerberos to choose men for the program.

Suspecting both the DOD and the CIA of involvement in Toby's disappearance had made Faith even more paranoid. To the point that simply leaving the cabin for this short trip to the bay had her jumping at shadows, although her instincts told her she'd escaped detection so far.

To avoid being tracked via facial recognition software run on security camera images, Faith had used the costuming skills she'd learned while acting in school plays during junior high and high school. Thankfully, she'd insisted that any safe house Toby set up contain a wide range of disguises for them both in case they needed to leave the cabin.

Thank you, Mrs. Kukei. The woman in charge of Faith's high school drama department had made certain all her actors became competent at changing their own appearances, whether through costuming or makeup. While Faith hadn't acted in years, she'd often used the techniques she'd learned in order to keep her identity hidden when under threat from foreign governments or other groups who hadn't wanted her to reveal the truth.

Today Faith had gone with a simple disguise. She wore an oversized, floppy hat that tied underneath her chin and hid all of her hair. Not only did the wide brim add shadows to her face, but the attached scarf covered her ears and jawline. Large sunglasses in tourist Day-Glo green protected her eyes.

"Okay. Here it is," Siobahn said. "Hmm...right. I went down to Fort Bragg to meet a contact while researching my article. As he was walking me back to my car, we caught sight of a group of special ops guys heading back to base from some mission in the woods. Before they realized we were within earshot, I overheard one of the men complain about their training exercise being cut short due to those freaky guys from Kerberos. I turned to my friend and asked him what Kerberos was, but he claimed not to recognize the name." Siobahn's loud, frustrated sigh made Faith smile.

"In fact," Siobahn continued, "everyone I asked after that either denied having heard of Kerberos or clammed up and told me to leave it alone because it was too dangerous. Since I couldn't find corroboration, I had to leave the name out of my article. Does that help?"

The hairs on the back of Faith's neck quivered. "Yes, I think so. A few of the missing military personnel Toby had been investigating were later seen in training exercises conducted by a secretive group of soldiers." Her brother had speculated that the members of that secret team had been experimental, super-human soldiers.

"Toby claimed that Kerberos is a top-secret black ops group run out of the CIA by Wayne Jamieson, the CIA's Director of In-House Projects."

"Figures the CIA would be involved."

"Yeah. Toby's notes indicated that Kerberos is Jamieson's private organization and hinted that not even his superiors at the CIA know the full reach of Kerberos. Toby heard rumors that Kerberos provides elite assassination squads and military units comprised mostly of graduates from the superhuman soldier program. But he hadn't been able to locate the program or determine who provided Kerberos's teams with assignments." If Faith could locate the freaks those soldiers at Fort Bragg had been talking about, maybe one of them would lead her to where Toby was being held.

"I wonder..." Siobahn said.

"What?" Faith heard the rustling of paper over the line.

"Four of the missing men in my article were found in remote towns near military bases. The men were crazed. Filled with such violent rage that a few observers suspected they were rabid."

Which matched what Toby had discovered. "You think maybe they got separated from a Kerberos team?" Faith asked. "If so, wouldn't someone have gone looking for them?"

"Not necessarily. The men had already been declared dead." Siobahn's voice vibrated with the energy that came from being on the trail of a juicy story. "If they really were part of Kerberos, by the time they ended up under observation by civilians, it would be too much of a risk for their commanding officers, if Kerberos even has such a thing, to claim them. Better to write them off as collateral damage, then go in and secretly destroy the records and the wayward men. Two of the missing men from my article were admitted to hospitals, one was taken to jail, and one was spotted by local law enforcement but eluded capture. Within a week, all the subjects were dead, their bodies gone, and no records left that they'd ever been found. Most of the people who had initial contact with the freaky men also died shortly after in suspicious accidents. The only reason I learned about what happened was that several of the first responders were scared into hiding. One of them later contacted me and put me in touch with the others. Through their statements, and thanks to copies of records a number of them had made, I was able to match identities of the men they'd seen to those from my list of military personnel who'd been declared dead."

Faith's heart sank. "Yes. That matches Toby's research. He found a few escapees. Based on their symptoms, and testimony from others involved in the scientific program, the treatment given to the men resulted in insanity and rage. None had survived their encounters with the outside world. Either they'd killed themselves or been killed when law enforcement tried to capture them." Her gut screamed that she was fast running out of time to find Toby. She wished his notes included some sort of timeline regarding how long men lasted in this program.

Did she have days? Weeks? Hours?

Faith bit her lip and shoved her fear for her brother aside. Siobahn's story only proved how severe a threat the men running Kerberos posed. She hated putting her friend further into danger, but she couldn't do this alone. "I need to talk with your contact at Fort Bragg."

"Faith, this was four months ago. Teams rotate in and out of there on a daily basis. The odds of the Kerberos team still being there are small. Besides, my friend isn't stationed at Fort Bragg any more. He was on a short-term assignment and is now working at the Pentagon. Without a contact on the inside, you'll never get the information you want."

Faith grinned. "That's why I have you. Ms. My-Dad-Is-A-Four-Star-General."

"Retired."

"Like that makes any difference."

"You're right. Dad could get you access. But with the heightened security in place these days, I don't think he can arrange for you to talk to people fast enough for what you need."

Faith ground her teeth, hating that her friend was right. "So what do you suggest, Siobahn? Because I'm at my wit's end. This is my brother's life I'm talking about. Think about how you'd react if one of your brothers went missing."

Siobahn sighed. "Tell you what, I'll ask Dad and my brothers if they've ever heard of Kerberos, freaky soldiers, or Wayne Jamieson. Have them discreetly put the word out. Okay?"

"Yes. Thanks. And Siobahn, please, be extra careful. Toby wouldn't have been easy to take down, yet they got him. I don't want you to go missing, too."

Her friend's deep, reckless laugh made Faith remember too late that warning Siobahn away from danger had always sent her running forward instead. "Never mind, it's not as if you pay any attention to personal safety when you're hot on a story," Faith grumbled, earning another laugh from Siobahn.

"Pot. Kettle," Siobahn pointed out. "You wouldn't be sticking your nose into this matter against your brother's advice if part of you didn't thrive on danger. You'd have turned the investigation over to the authorities if you wanted to stay safe. Maybe now you'll finally realize that you were born to be a journalist. I want you back on the team when this is all over."

"Siobahn," Faith said, lacing the word with exasperation.

"I'm serious, kiddo. Think about it. I'll call when I can. Ciao."

"How is he doing?" Dr. Leonard Kaufmann asked his lead scientist as he nodded toward the room where Toby Andrews was being given another injection of the drugs that would open him to mind control.

"His extensive training on how to resist torture has been a difficult obstacle to overcome, sir. However, it appears that we have finally found the right combination of physical torture and poisons to weaken him so that our drugs can break through his resistance."

"Excellent." Kaufmann had been reluctant to add the former military intelligence officer to the program. Not only because of the man's training, but because as an officer, the man was used to being an authority figure. The men who adapted easiest to the mind control protocols were those in subordinate positions who already had an innate need to please their commanders.

Still, as he'd proven with SSU agent Rafe Andros, it was possible to break down an unsuitable prospect and turn him into an obedient soldier. All that was required was to find the correct key for breaking the subject's spirit. Then conditioning proceeded at the usual rate.

Now, if only the scientists could control the rages and put a stop to the physical deterioration that rendered his soldiers useless after three or four months, they'd have a highly profitable commodity to sell on the international market. He really would need to ask Jamieson about capturing Dr. Montague and returning her to the program. She'd been so close to making a breakthrough. But she'd fled after discovering the true reason he needed her research.

With the anniversary demonstration for the President coming up soon, he needed all the enhanced soldiers he could create. Those already in the field would have deteriorated past the point of peak effectiveness by the time of the demonstration. Having Dr. Montague back would not only hopefully lead to the stability he required, but from what he understood, the woman had been given access to the research data from Dr.

Nevsky's microchip. Data which would allow Kaufmann to further refine his formula.

He scowled. His former boss should have trusted him with the backup data from the superhuman soldier program, instead of implanting the chip in his daughter's abdomen. It had taken two years after Nevsky's death for the microchip to be found, but it had ended up in the hands of the do-gooder Surgical Strike Unit instead of Kerberos. Leaving Kaufmann struggling to catch up to where Nevsky had been before his death.

Andrews's scream filtered through the examination room door. Kaufmann shook his head. That was another aspect of the program he'd have to work on. The pain of the drugs hitting the bloodstream resulted in agonizing screams. Since he intended to set up clinics in regular hospitals and office buildings in order to turn out his custom made soldiers, spies and assassins, he didn't want to have to soundproof all his rooms.

"Tell me, doctor," he began, taking the scientist's arm and leading him away from Andrews's room. "Will you have Andrews ready in time to participate in the President's demonstration?"

The man glanced back at the room just as Andrews gave another piercing shriek of agony. Nodding thoughtfully, the scientist replied, "Yes. It sounds as if his resistance is breaking as planned. I do believe he will be ready in time."

"Excellent."

CHAPTER TWO

Four Days Later
A Small Tourist Town on the Chesapeake Bay

FAITH SANK BACK into the shadows of the alley, staying hidden while she watched the restaurant where Wayne Jamieson was having dinner.

Even she had to admit that being here tonight was one of the more rash moves of her life. When Toby included a photo, background and daily schedule information for Jamieson in his notes, he'd probably never imagined that one day his sister would start following the man. But Faith had reached a new level of desperation.

Her inquiries had hit nothing but brick walls.

She had a lot of valuable data, but no smoking gun to bring down Kerberos or help her locate her brother. The people she'd talked to either had never heard of Kerberos, refused to acknowledge they'd ever heard the name despite every indication to the contrary, or knew the name and had nothing but a few rumors to add.

Siobahn's investigation had also ground to a halt. Her father and brothers claimed not to have heard of Kerberos or Jamieson. Even her contact who'd overheard the reference to the freaky soldiers at Fort Bragg refused to discuss the group any further.

Unable to think of any other way to get the data she needed, Faith had started following Jamieson, using the training Toby had given her on how to covertly follow a target. Unfortunately, Jamieson was paranoid and always traveled with several bodyguards.

Because she was naturally messy—her hair never stayed neatly confined no matter how tightly she braided it or how much hairspray she used—Faith knew she more resembled a dazed hippie than a focused assassin. So she'd kept her disguises artsy and disheveled. The few times she'd passed within view of Jamieson's bodyguards, they'd given her an initial sharply assessing glance, then moved on. Even so, they were well-trained and wary of anyone getting within striking distance of their boss. Once, a teenager on a skateboard had veered to within a few feet of Jamieson as the man was being hustled by the guards between his car and an office building. Faith had watched in horror as the guards spotted the teenager and reached for their guns. Luckily, the sidewalk had been busy and the guards hadn't actually pulled out their weapons, just kept their hands inside their jacket pockets until the oblivious boy changed direction and sped away.

Still, it had served as a warning not to get too close. Which was frustrating the hell out of Faith. She needed to catch Jamieson engaged either in conversation or in action that tied him to Toby and the missing personnel. Breaking into his office at the CIA was out of the question. His home security was beyond her ability to crack, although she had no doubt that her brother could have broken into Jamieson's house. She'd gone so far as to buy an electronic listening device at a spy store, but hadn't been able to get close enough to Jamieson to plant it on him.

Having followed Jamieson for several days, she recognized that he was too dangerous for her to confront. But tonight, an elegantly handsome man with dark hair and eyes had greeted Jamieson as the CIA director exited his chauffeured town car. After a curt nod to the stranger and a quick glance around the deserted parking lot, Jamieson strode into the restaurant with an arrogance that indicated he clearly expected his visitor to follow. Which he had.

Faith hoped the other man would be an easier target. She fingered Toby's pistol in her pocket, and tamped down her nerves and the revulsion at being in possession of a gun again. But desperation left her no choice.

Still, she hoped she wouldn't have to shoot. Her plan was to get Jamieson's companion alone and question him about Kerberos. Hopefully, the man would be able to provide information that would lead her to where Toby was being held.

If not, then... She blew out a breath. Well, she really didn't want to think past that. She'd rather wonder if the men were right now discussing Kerberos and the fate of more innocent men. If she stormed in there waving her gun and demanded to know where Toby was, would she see surprise on their faces? Or scorn?

Of course, a face-to-face showdown with Jamieson would be suicidal. He'd have her killed before she could speak her first word. So she'd resigned herself to lurking until Jamieson's companion exited the restaurant.

And prayed that he had the answers she needed.

"Hold it right there."

The young woman who stepped out of the shadows was the

last person Mark Tonelli would expect to hold a gun on him. As his eyes flicked over her generously curved, petite body and her wildly curling, dark red hair that spilled from beneath a tribal print scarf, all he could think of was that he was being mugged by a woman who looked like a first grade art teacher.

A very pissed off, yet very sexy first grade art teacher. She wore a gauzy, patchwork skirt over black and green striped leggings that bagged slightly at the ankles, and thick-soled, ugly shoes. He would have thought her a homeless person, except that her clothes appeared to be clean and in excellent condition.

Which, given the way his body had jolted into sexual awareness the second he heard her voice, was a good thing. He would not allow himself to lust after a transient. No matter how sweet yet sexy her voice sounded.

Mark frowned at the direction of his thoughts. He didn't find untidy women attractive. He liked sleek, sophisticated women. But he couldn't deny that he was turned on by this young woman wearing, of all things, a thick hand knit cardigan that sprouted tissues from its pockets. He couldn't stop staring in fascination at the place where the buttons strained to keep the edges of the sweater together, forming a gap between her breasts that he desperately wanted to investigate.

He shook his head. What the hell was wrong with him? It was dark. He'd just been chewed out by his boss, CIA Director of In-House Projects Wayne Jamieson. He had better things to do than stare at this woman's chest. Like get her to put the damn gun away. And move her out of sight of the restaurant entrance before Jamieson and his guards exited.

Her hand shook from supporting the weight of the pistol—a Glock 21 that was much too heavy and too big for her small hand—and he didn't trust her not to accidentally shoot him. *Amateur.*

The thought lacked his usual bite when considering those

less skilled than himself. He must be more tired than he realized. That was the only logical explanation he could give as to why he hadn't already disarmed her.

You haven't disarmed her, a voice deep inside him commented, *because you're too busy being enchanted with her.*

Mark scowled. It was true. He wanted to knock the gun away, then scoop her up in his arms and take her someplace safe.

Protective instincts? Him?

He glanced back at the elegant brick facade of the restaurant. Had Jamieson slipped something into his drink that was affecting his mood? Or was this another side effect of the changes brought on by what he'd witnessed in Dr. Ivanov's lab in Moscow?

The nose of the gun prodded his side and Mark turned, his lips twitching in amusement at the woman's courage.

Or stupidity.

She nudged him again. "Start walking." She nodded her head toward the dark mouth of the alley between the restaurant and the closed women's boutique next door.

"Why?" he asked.

She didn't pretend to misunderstand his question. "Because you're one of Jamieson's associates," she snarled, sounding more like a punk teenager with an attitude than a first grade teacher. "I can't get past his bodyguards, so you'll have to do."

Mark narrowed his eyes in speculation, reassessing his opinion of her. Intelligence. Determination. And an all-too-familiar bitterness that came from a personal wrong not yet righted.

"Do for what?" he demanded.

"Walk." She nudged him again with her gun.

"Oh, for pity's sake." With an abrupt, impatient movement Mark knocked the hand holding the gun aside, then plucked the weapon from her lax fingers. He pocketed the weapon and took her arm. "Let's talk." But instead of taking her toward the alley, he led her toward his car.

She jerked back, trying to break his hold. "Wait! What are you doing?"

Mark just dug his fingers deeper into her arm, hitting a pressure point that would cause her enough pain to obey him, and yanked her forward. "You're coming with me."

"I most certainly am not!"

Mark could hear the fear in her voice, mixed with bewilderment over how easily he'd taken control. Still, he rolled his eyes when she planted her feet and leaned back, forcing him to stop or risk making a scene.

Grabbing both her arms, he leaned down until he was almost nose-to-nose with her. And tried to ignore her tantalizing sugar-cookie-and-cinnamon scent. "Listen," he said with barely concealed impatience. "You're the one who wanted to talk badly enough to hold a gun on me. Well, it's not safe to talk here."

He inclined his head toward the club. "Jamieson will be coming out soon. Do you really want him to see us together?"

She slanted an uneasy glance back toward the restaurant. The woman was well informed if she understood that Jamieson was the more dangerous man.

For some reason, he wanted to soothe her fear away with a kiss. But then she flattened her lips and notched up her chin. "Just because I don't want to be caught here by Jamieson doesn't mean I'm stupid enough to get in a car with you."

Mark stared at her. Didn't she realize that he held all the power? He had her gun, for God's sake. But instead of reminding her of that fact, he found himself saying, "I'm not the danger, woman. I would have hurt you by now if that was my intent. But since you know his name, you're a threat to

Jamieson. You're going to come with me and tell me everything you know. Then I'll protect you."

"Protect me? No, thanks. I can take care of myself."

Mark snorted in disgust and shook his head. "Right." He tugged her toward the car. This time she didn't resist. "That's why I disarmed you so easily." He shot her a glance out of the corner of his eye and saw something like chagrin cross her face.

"You've never even used a gun, have you?" he guessed.

"Yes, actually, I have," she said. "I just...loathe...guns."

There was a wealth of complex emotions behind that comment. Grief. Hatred. A tinge of guilt.

But the grief was what interested him the most.

"It doesn't matter. No one would take you seriously in that outfit," he commented. Not true. If she'd held the gun like a pro he would have considered her a threat even if she'd been stark naked.

Or, given his reaction to her clothed body, maybe that was an incorrect assessment.

He caught her grin out of the corner of his eye, then turned so he could feel the full impact of it head-on. It was like being hit by a super nova. The skin around her coffee brown eyes crinkled and her cheeks developed a lovely dimple.

"That's the point," she replied, tucking a few of the tissues back into her pockets. "This is an earthy, quirky neighborhood. I'd look more out of place in an ordinary pair of jeans than this hodgepodge of an outfit."

Well, at least she admitted the outfit was a poor fashion statement. But Mark wouldn't have cared if she wore a neon green sack, if he could just get her to aim another one of those smiles at him.

"Your expensive suit doesn't fit in here at all," she commented. "But then, everyone who comes to this restaurant stands out."

Mark figured Jamieson had chosen the location because it was in a small, touristy town neither man would normally visit. Yet the woman had a point. During the day their business attire would stand out from the tourists and bizarre locals.

Thank heavens it was night and so late that this end of the street was deserted. Except for him and his would-be kidnapper.

"You look like a high school librarian," he said, sensing that saying she really resembled a first grade teacher would not earn him any points. "Not a killer. Anyone with a brain could see you don't have the stomach to kill." He shot her a look. "Which makes me wonder why you held a gun on me if you're so afraid of them. Did you really plan on killing me if I didn't cooperate?"

"Of course not," she huffed with a feminine toss of her head that sent thick, curling ribbons of hair spilling out of her ponytail.

He could not believe he was getting hard because of this messy woman. Yet he couldn't remember the last time he'd had such a strong, *honest* reaction to a woman.

"I just wanted to scare you into talking to me," she added.

Mark beeped his navy blue BMW unlocked and shoved her into the passenger seat. As he slid behind the wheel, the restaurant door opened. "Duck down," Mark ordered.

"What? Why?" She twisted in her seat to look out the back window.

Infuriating woman. He pushed on her shoulder to lower her head below the windows just as one of Jamieson's guards looked their way.

"Stay down or Jamieson's men will get a good look at you and you'll be on their kill list." Mark accelerated slowly out of the parking lot as if he hadn't noticed the group of men at the restaurant door.

The woman made a sound of frustration, but scooted down until she was tucked under the dashboard. "Kill list? Why? I haven't made any threat against Jamieson, so why would they want me dead?"

Only when he'd driven two blocks with no sign of being followed did he bother to answer her question. "They're loyal to Jamieson and he's very paranoid. Plus, he doesn't entirely trust me right now. Anyone seen with me will be considered either a potential threat or a potential lever to get me to behave. And no one who knows me would ever think you'd matter enough to be leverage."

After a heavy silence, during which he wondered if he'd managed to insult the woman, she asked, "Can I sit up now?"

He checked their surroundings. This nearly deserted street would soon dead end into the beach access road. Per his earlier reconnaissance, there were several wooded stretches along the beach where he could pull over. Since the two other cars on the road were headed in the opposite direction, Mark told his passenger, "Yes, you can sit up."

The woman scrambled into the seat. Mark forced himself to look away as her clothing pulled tight. But when her arm accidentally brushed against his shoulder, a sexual jolt shot straight to his groin.

"So. Are you CIA, too?" she asked.

He considered lying to her, but didn't see the point. "Yes. Jamieson is my boss."

Her face paled and for a second he thought she was going to try and jump out of the car. But then she squared her shoulders and settled against the seat back.

Mark wanted to pull her into his arms and tell her that he was one of the good guys and would protect her from Jamieson. But the truth was that he'd been skirting the line between right and wrong for a very long time without concern for anything but achieving his revenge. His urge to keep this woman safe threatened that mission.

He didn't understand this new side of himself and he certainly did not like being guided by emotion rather than reason.

"So, if Jamieson is your boss, why doesn't he trust you?"

"Because he ordered my father killed." Even after four days, Mark was still reeling from that discovery. He'd thought he'd killed everyone involved in the kidnapping and torture that led to his father's death. But then he'd seen his father's good luck charm —a tiny, bronze, Etruscan horse—on Jamieson's desk. And he'd known he'd been played. Jamieson had ordered his father's death.

"Jamieson doesn't know if I've figured it out yet and am secretly working against him," Mark continued, "which I am, or if I'm clueless and really as loyal an employee as I've led him to believe."

The woman didn't answer, but Mark felt her eyes on him. Weighing his statement. Probably debating whether or not she could believe him.

For the first time in a very long while, it mattered that someone believe in him. A dangerous thought, particularly since he should be solely focused on determining if she could be used as a tool in his fight against Jamieson. Instead, he wanted her trust for entirely personal reasons.

Fool.

After checking again to make certain Jamieson's body-guards hadn't followed them, Mark turned the car onto the beach access road. There was a secluded picnic area not far from here that would allow them to talk without the car being spotted.

And it was a perfect place to make out.

Enough with the sex thoughts! Mark resisted the urge to check his image in the rearview mirror to see if he had an unexplained lump on his head. Something was causing his libido to go crazy and he was damned if he accepted that this odd woman had such power over him. But his reflection showed no contusions or other abnormalities. Leaving him only one conclusion regarding his strange behavior.

I must be losing my mind.

CHAPTER THREE

FAITH'S STOMACH did a nervous little flip-flop when the elegant, mysterious man pulled the car onto a sandy road that curved out of view into a stand of pines. Oddly enough, her gut told her she was safe with him. And while she might not have been honing her instincts lately by reporting from the war-torn countries of the world, dealing with teenagers kept her truth-and-danger-meter in prime condition.

This sexy, arrogant man definitely seemed more annoyed by her than angry. Hell, he'd even said he wanted to protect her. He'd obviously assumed that because her hand shook when she'd held the gun she wasn't used to violence. The truth was the opposite. Her assignments overseas had toughened her to the point that it had been routine for her to carry a knife or gun on her person even when running to the grocery.

But if appearing weak and helpless got this man to tell her what she wanted, good. She'd just ignore the traitorous heat spiraling in her belly from his presence. And she'd pretend she didn't notice how the scent of his rich, musky cologne filled the car, making her skin heat as if he were touching her instead of sitting a foot away.

She'd also ignore how his dark hair lay in hair-sprayed perfection, making her want nothing more than to separate the thick strands with her fingers, messing his hair up and marking him as hers.

Whoa. What?

He was one of the bad guys. Maybe not quite as bad as Wayne Jamieson, true. She couldn't imagine Jamieson saying he wanted to protect her. If the ruthless CIA director learned she'd been following him, he'd swat her away like an annoying fly and order his bodyguard to kill her. But even if this man seemed less dangerous, she had absolutely no business picturing herself acting on this crazy attraction.

He was her best lead for finding her missing brother. That was all that mattered.

And yet...when he stopped the car her stupid heart fluttered in anticipation, nervous as a teenager on a date with her hot crush.

But he didn't turn his body toward her or reach for her hand. Instead, he flicked her a glance she couldn't interpret, then stared out the windshield. She bit her lip, swallowing disappointment and calling herself a fool for wanting attention from this man when, for more years than she could count, she hadn't wanted the bother of dealing with a relationship.

"How did you come to be outside that restaurant?" he demanded. "Who were you following?"

"Not you," she reassured him, sensing that his ego wouldn't accept any other answer. Luckily, she was telling the truth. "I followed Jamieson. The one who's in charge of Kerberos."

His head jerked toward her. Even in the dimly lit interior of the car she saw his eyes flash with alarm, then fury. "How did you hear about Kerberos?"

There was danger in his tone. Maybe even death. But nothing was going to stop her from finding her brother.

The man's eyes bored into her, reminding her that he was

waiting for an answer. She frowned. This wasn't how the evening was supposed to turn out. The plan had been for her to question him. Not the other way around.

Suddenly it didn't seem such a good idea to be sitting here in the dark with this stranger. He was one of Jamieson's colleagues. True, this was the first time she'd seen him with Jamieson, but that didn't make him innocent. After all, she'd only been following Jamieson for a few days, so she didn't know how close the two men were. For all she knew, once the stranger finished questioning her, he'd kill her.

Panicked, she grabbed for the door handle.

The man exhaled, the sound one of patience reaching its end. "Stop trying to run away and just tell me what's going on. I am *not* going to hurt you."

"Right. You're going to protect me," she shot back, letting sarcasm drip from her words. Yet her hand stilled on the door handle.

His eyes narrowed, but to her surprise he didn't deny it. Which for some reason caused her heart to flutter.

And whether it was her libido talking, or some other part of her, a little voice pointed out that regardless of whether she could fully trust him or not, she had little choice but to cooperate. She needed answers. Toby had already been missing for nearly five weeks. She didn't believe in psychic visions, but for the past couple of days her dreams had been full of blood, death and a driving sense of urgency. Each morning she awoke exhausted and filled with dread.

Wherever Toby had disappeared to, she need to find him. Fast.

"Woman, I don't have all night. Will you *please* answer my question? Where did you hear the name Kerberos?"

"My name isn't woman," she grumbled, even though for some strange reason hearing this man call her woman turned her on. "It's Faith. Faith Andrews. Who are you?"

He hesitated, but not with recognition of her name. Good. Instead she suspected he was trying to decide if he wanted to tell her the truth or not. "*Hey mister* has a nice ring to it," she offered.

His eyebrows lifted in astonishment. Okay, yeah. This wasn't exactly the type of situation that invited teasing. But she often resorted to humor when she was nervous. Or in danger.

"Mark," he finally admitted. "My name is Mark...Tonelli."

She opened her mouth to say something smart alecky, but a slight hardening of his expression had her biting her tongue.

"Kerberos?" he prompted.

Faith sighed. Was she really going to confide in a total stranger? Why? Because he claimed to be working against Jamieson? Because he used the word please and hadn't hurt her, or even been angry with her for holding a gun on him? Because he was the sexiest man she'd met in months?

No. Because I'm desperate and if there's even the slightest chance he can help me, I have to take it.

"Okay, Mark. Before I tell you anything, I want your promise that after I'm done you'll answer my questions."

He studied her for so long, her cheeks grew warm under his scrutiny. What did he see? Did he find her attractive? Think her a fool? She clenched her teeth and reminded herself again that it didn't matter what he thought, as long as he gave her the answers to help her save Toby. Still, she wished they had met when she wasn't wearing a wig and colored contacts.

Just when she thought he wasn't going to answer, he gave a curt nod.

"Okay." She turned and stared out the windshield at the moonlight shimmering on the incoming waves. "My brother Toby is with military intelligence," she began. "Several months ago, he started an investigation that kept him more out of touch than usual. He'd warned me of this ahead of time and promised to check in every two weeks to our secure email account. When he missed two check-ins in a row, I started to worry."

She plucked at the hem of her sweater. "Then I received a package in the mail. From Toby. With a letter, a bunch of hand-written and typed notes, and two flash drives. In the letter, he explained that he'd instructed the lawyer to send the package out if he hadn't checked in for four weeks."

Faith shivered, despite her thick sweater. She hated thinking about her brother being in pain. Tortured.

"The flash drives held all the details of his unofficial investigation into missing military and law enforcement personnel. He'd traced several of the men back to an organization called Kerberos. And he pointed to Wayne Jamieson at the CIA as the head of Kerberos."

Mark didn't say a word, but she felt his increased tension.

"Toby had been closing in on Jamieson before he disappeared. In his notes were details on the man's schedule, where his office was located, his home address, everything I needed to start following him."

Mark snorted in disbelief. "Right."

She raised her brows. "Looks can be deceiving, as I'm sure you know." At first glance, Mark could be a model out of *Town and Country*. Only once you moved close enough to see the hard look in his eyes would you understand he was a tough, dangerous man.

"I used to be a damn good investigative journalist," she said. "Our team even won a Pulitzer." Not that they'd been after the prize during their investigation. No, all they'd wanted was to expose the truth. But mentioning the award did have a way of garnering instant respect.

"I know how to gather information without being discovered," she continued. "Jamieson isn't the first highly guarded target I've followed. I make sure that when his bodyguards do spot me, they see a completely harmless woman."

"Now that I can believe," Mark muttered.

"Yes, you've already expressed how threatening you find me." She'd often used her appearance to put people off guard. Her curly blonde hair, short and curvy stature, and big blue eyes often lulled subjects into thinking she was a ditzy blonde. Only later, when her story ran, did they realize they'd given away more than they'd intended.

However, in the eighteen months since she'd given up her career, she'd made an effort to be a strong role model for the female high school and college girls she taught. To her surprise, it annoyed her that Mark had bought into the ditzy female routine, even though that had been her goal. Her pride wanted him to recognize her intelligence. See her more as an equal than a person to be ignored.

Squelching those thoughts, she said firmly, "Your opinion of me doesn't matter."

Liar. You want him to like you. Respect you.

Desire you.

Faith ignored the voice in her head. "I want to find the place where Kerberos keeps the personnel they've kidnapped. Because I'm convinced Toby isn't dead. I'm afraid they took him to wherever it is that they create their enhanced soldiers." She didn't think they would have put Toby into their program yet. They'd need him to confirm all the locations where he'd stored his research and every person who'd received copies of his notes. Even then, she wasn't certain if they'd put Toby into the program, or just kill him.

Mark's lips thinned and a muscle next to his left eye started twitching, setting all her instincts into high alert. "What do you know about Kerberos?" she asked.

At the same instant, Mark snapped, "Tell me everything you've learned about the enhanced soldiers."

She crossed her arms over her chest and stared him down.

"No. You first. Prove you really want to help me. Otherwise, I'm out of here."

He raised an eyebrow.

"What? You don't think I could escape from you?" she asked.

The corner of his mouth lifted in disdain.

"You caught me unawares before. So what? I'm prepared now."

"I'd like to see you try."

There was something sensual beneath the threat that held Faith immobile. Then she shook her head. "Don't worry, I'm not leaving until you give me the information I need. So talk."

After a long, probing look that made her want to squirm in her seat, Mark turned his attention back to the ocean. Finally, he spoke. "Kerberos is Wayne Jamieson's private black ops group." When he glanced over at her to check that she understood, Faith nodded.

"Kerberos specializes in assassinations and other actions the government can't publicly take credit for."

"But...I thought Kerberos ran teams of enhanced soldiers."

Mark looked away, but not before Faith saw the bleakness in his eyes. "Yes, now it does. But Kerberos initially started out with squads of normal men. Men who'd met strict physical and mental requirements and believed wholeheartedly in the organization's mission. A few years ago, Kerberos started funding a lab doing research to create a superhuman soldier. The methods used to transform the men are quite...painful...and ultimately fatal."

No. Oh, no. "What do you mean, fatal?" Toby's notes had mentioned that the escapees had all died, but that seemed to be a result of confrontations with law enforcement. He hadn't mentioned anything about the long-term effects of the program beyond the insane rages.

"The drugs involved eventually cause madness and death by massive organ failure."

Remnants of her nightmares beat against her mind. Pictures of Toby bleeding to death. Screaming in pain. She sucked in a sharp breath and dug her nails into her palms, focusing on the small pain to force back the images. "How long —" Her voice broke and she had to clear her throat or risk crying. "How long until the subjects die?"

"A few months after treatment is started."

Faith's stomach unknotted itself. "Toby has been missing only a little over a month. Even if..." She cleared her throat. "Even if they break from their established criteria and put Toby in the program, he still has time."

"Maybe. Maybe not. There are rumors of a new, accelerated program in progress," Mark added. "With perhaps a quicker rise to standards and then a quicker decline."

She bit her lip and crossed her arms over her chest as her stomach took a nosedive.

"Of course, you don't know that Jamieson ordered your brother kidnapped. He might not be in danger of becoming one of the altered soldiers."

Was that actually sympathy she heard in his voice? The chill that had settled over her at the thought of Toby becoming a victim of the program slowly thawed.

"What do you know about the selection process?" Mark asked.

Faith shrugged. "Toby had a list of criteria for subjects." She explained about the different parameters and why she believed her independent brother didn't fit their need for subservient men. "Do you think they'd break precedent and add Toby to their roster?"

"I don't know. I'm not privy to that side of the program." He stared out the window and Faith couldn't read his mood. Was he processing what she'd said? Planning to kill her?

"Where are you staying?" He made it more of a demand than a question.

She blinked at the abrupt change of subject. "That's none of your business."

"Yes, it is. I've been working to take down Kerberos and Jamieson from the inside. Your brother's information will help me achieve that. I need to keep you safe from Jamieson in the meantime."

"I can take care of myself."

He gave her a condescending little smile. "Not good enough. You'll stay at my safe house."

"Excuse me? I may have confided in you, but that doesn't put you in charge of my personal safety. You're still a stranger and I don't fully trust you. I'm safer on my own."

"No, you are not. I can't guarantee that Jamieson's guards didn't get a good look at you back at the restaurant."

She shrugged. When he frowned over her lack of concern, she bit back a smug smile.

Mark's eyes narrowed and he studied her with new intensity.

"Is that your real hair?"

He reached out to touch it, but she knocked his hand away. He let his hand drop, and she wondered if she imagined the flare of disappointment in his eyes. She hoped he hadn't been able to read on her face the anticipation she'd felt as his hand moved toward her. The longing to feel his touch had been so powerful, it had scared her common sense into reasserting itself.

"Again. None of your business."

"Faith, Jamieson would kill you just for knowing about Kerberos. Kill you twice for knowing he's the force behind the program. The best way to bring him down is to work together. In order to do that, I need to make sure you're staying where he can't find you. I have a safe house you can use."

"*You* have a safe house? Not the CIA?"

He tapped his fingers against the steering wheel. "Should something happen to turn my colleagues against me, I want someplace to hide that they don't know about."

"Hmm..." The similarity to her brother's thinking regarding the need for an escape plan made her trust Mark a little more. Still, she had no intention of staying where he could find her. For all she knew, as soon as she was out of sight he'd call up Jamieson and order her killed. "My answer is still no."

He glared at her, but she was beginning to think he was all bluster. Or maybe she just wanted to believe that what she saw behind his eyes was concern. Totally unrealistic given the fact that she'd barely known him—she glanced at the dashboard clock—more than an hour. Yet her instincts said she could push him on this.

So she simply stared back at him, brows lifted to let him know she wasn't giving in.

His mouth flattened, but he broke the stare first and looked toward the ocean. Faith waited while he worked his jaw side to side, struggling with some emotion.

"Did your brother leave you proof?"

It wasn't the response she'd expected. "Proof of what?" she asked carefully.

"Of Jamieson's connection to Kerberos and the missing men."

"He has copies of e-mails from a couple of people inside the DOD giving Jamieson a list of suitable men, but without any mention of what the list is for. There's no mention of Kerberos. He also has recent autopsy and police reports on military and law enforcement men who had supposedly died months earlier. Plus statements connecting a few of the missing men to 'freaky' teams of soldiers running exercises on some of the military bases. A lot of circumstantial stuff. Enough to cause trouble and maybe spark further investigation if I sent it to my media contacts. But that's not what I want."

Mark turned and speared her with a look. "What do you want?"

You. Ugh. Why did her libido have to choose tonight to come roaring back? Was her sudden desire to kiss him a result of adrenaline? A desperate attempt to find a point of security in this dangerous situation?

Maybe it's just chemistry.

Uh-huh. Right.

She cleared her throat. "To find Toby and bring him home. Will you help me?"

"If you want me to save your brother, I'll need to see his notes."

Faith shook her head. "No way. I don't trust you that far."

Mark looked down his nose at her. He honest-to-God pulled the aristocratic, arrogant expression off. And looked sexy doing it.

But he didn't sway her. For all she knew, he was just gathering as much information as he could before turning her over to Jamieson.

"I promise you. Work with me to bring down Jamieson and Kerberos and I will help you find your brother. Just give me a copy of the damn notes."

"I'll think about it."

After so many days of hiding, trusting no one except Siobahn as she moved closer to Jamieson, Mark's cooperation seemed too good a shot of luck to believe.

Toby's notes were someplace safe. Some *places* safe, that is. She'd left copies with a variety of friends around the world, all with different instructions on what to do with them if she died. That didn't mean she wasn't going to protect her own copy. Limited trust was the plan until she figured out his true intentions.

She smiled at him and tried not to freak out that she was on a deserted beach with no way to get back to civilization on her own without walking.

As if reading her thoughts, he said, "You still consider me a threat? After all I've told you?" He sounded offended, which only made her smile grow.

"Yep."

"You are the most infuriating woman." Before Faith had any clue regarding his intention, he twisted in his seat, grabbed her head, and kissed her.

Instant heat spread through her body, but before Faith could pull him closer, he lifted his head and sat back in his seat. Arousal warred with disappointment and confusion as she watched him start the car.

"I have no plans to harm you or to bring you to Jamieson's attention," Mark snapped as he drove back toward the center of the small town. "For some reason I find myself extremely attracted to you and am feeling strongly possessive." He shot her an annoyed glance, as if she'd done something to ensnare him against his will. "I'd rather take you home with me, but I'll settle for taking you to the safe house."

"No."

Being alone with him had now become dangerous on an entirely new level. She wanted another taste of him. Wanted to touch him and feel his hands on her naked flesh. But it was too much. Too soon.

Damn him, she didn't have time to be attracted to him.

When he started to protest, she put a hand on his thigh. "Mark, I have a safe place to stay tonight." She suspected he wouldn't approve of the beachside hostel and its young, hippy clientele. But she'd fit right in. And she doubted Jamieson or Mark would look for her in such a public place.

"Just drop me anywhere on Main Street and I'll be fine."

"I—"

"And don't try to follow me."

He glared at her again. For some reason, that only made her hot.

"It's dangerous for me to be seen with you," she reminded him. "Give me a secure way to contact you. After you give me some sort of a sign that you're actually working toward finding Toby, we can arrange a time to meet later in the week."

His fingers tensed on the steering wheel. "If you feel any sense of threat," he snapped as he pulled alongside the sidewalk, "you call me immediately."

"Agreed." Plenty of people were still milling about, enjoying the balmy evening. They'd give her cover and help her disappear faster.

To her surprise, he leaned over and gave her another hard, possessive kiss. Then, just as abruptly, he sat back. "Go. Before I decide to keep you here whether you want it or not."

Blinking in surprise, Faith let herself out of the car. Still reeling from the impact of the kiss, she watched him drive away. Then she shook her head and vanished into the crowd.

TWO AND A HALF HOURS LATER, Mark let himself into his apartment. So much for being clever. He'd been so proud of himself for slipping a tiny tracking device into Faith's sweater pocket when he'd kissed her. After dropping her at an all night coffee shop in the center of the small bayside town, he'd quickly found a place to park, then followed her on foot.

But within half an hour not only had he lost visual on her, he'd lost the signal. She must have found the device and destroyed it. Making him wonder just what kind of training she'd had.

He tossed his keys into the ebony bowl sitting on the teak side table, then turned and looked at his reflection in the gold and black inlaid mirror.

Hmm. He still looked the same. Brown hair, brown eyes. Aristocratic face showing no more than mild puzzlement. Shaking his head, he walked toward the living room, examining his hands as he went. He desperately needed a drink, but even his hands showed nothing of his inner turmoil. There wasn't a tremor to be found.

He poured himself a shot of vodka and threw it back.

The burn down his throat made him feel more like himself, instead of the aroused, possessive stranger he'd turned into the second he'd laid eyes on Miss Faith Andrews. For God's sake, she possessed information that might help him nail Jamieson, and all he could think of was how soon he could get her into bed.

This wasn't him. He didn't let his emotions dictate to him. He was civilized. Logical. Controlled.

Of course you are. That's why you kidnapped Susana Dias last month. You were dreaming of a life with her at your side. You were star-struck.

Mark frowned and poured another shot. Jamieson had ordered him to kidnap former supermodel Susana Dias because, during an appendectomy, a microchip containing critical research had been implanted into her stomach. But the moment Mark had met Susana, he'd felt like an awkward teenager. He'd been so overcome by her vibrant beauty that all he could think of was making her his own.

In hindsight, what he'd felt had been the need to possess a pretty object, thus improving his status.

With Faith, however, he'd been someone else entirely. Someone he didn't know. She brought him to full arousal just being near her, making him want to taste her again and again until she became a part of him. But it went beyond physical need. He wanted to get to know her better. To listen to her talk and to touch her skin and see how soft it might be. He wanted to protect her.

All that and he'd scarcely known the woman more than a couple of hours.

He'd heard of men falling in love at first sight. Was that what had happened to him? God, he hoped not. This was the worst possible time for him to become distracted. If he was going to be successful in bringing Jamieson down, he had to use all his wits and tread with extreme caution.

He glanced down and realized that he didn't know if this was his third or fourth glass of vodka. When had he stopped counting?

Not really caring, he shrugged and threw back what was in his glass. Then he set the glass aside and headed upstairs to his bedroom before he did something really stupid, like get drunk.

Although how there could be anything stupider than falling for an unknown like Faith Andrews, he didn't know.

She could be a plant from Jamieson, meant to trick him into betraying his true agenda.

Mark considered that a moment, then tossed the idea aside along with his necktie. His years as a street kid in Moscow and his eventual move into the upper levels of the intelligence community had taught him how to read people.

Every instinct told him Faith was telling the truth. And that she was equally attracted to him. The beginnings of a smug smile teased at his lips as he finished stripping.

The game he was playing with Jamieson had him riding an adrenaline high. He felt more alive than he had in years. But after meeting Faith, he realized that part of him had still been sleeping.

He wondered idly if this newfound sense of power and freedom was how addicts felt during a high. Had heroic knights experienced this delicious anticipation when tasked with quests from their ladies?

And Faith had given him a task, hadn't she? Still suspicious, she'd refused to turn over her notes until he gave her proof that he was searching for Toby. Which meant he needed deeper access to Kerberos's files.

He stepped into the double-headed shower enclosure and turned the water on hot.

Knowing that Jamieson was watching him, knowing that his boss must be wondering if Mark had made the connection between Jamieson and his father's death, meant he had to plan every move down to the last detail, including what he'd say should he be caught. While he knew a fair amount about computer hacking—any spy these days working among businessmen had better be prepared to steal secrets off a computer—he didn't possess the skills necessary to break through the level of security Jamieson would have in place.

If luck was with him, though, he might not have to call for help hacking Jamieson's computer. Over the past several days Jamieson had made it clear that he wanted Mark to take a more active role in Kerberos. He suspected it wasn't an indication of trust, but Jamieson's way of ensuring he'd be a viable scapegoat if the program came under scrutiny.

For now he was willing to play along. He needed concrete proof that Jamieson had ordered certain military and law enforcement men to be diverted against their will into Kaufmann's lab, turned into enhanced soldiers, then sent on assignment by Kerberos.

And he needed to find out whether or not Faith's brother had been among those men.

Mark hated that Faith had refused to stay at his safe house. She had no idea how uncharacteristic his offer had been. He was not good at sharing. Particularly when his safety or comfort were involved. Despite Faith being a stranger, and therefore a potential risk, his preference had actually been to bring her home with him. Which would have been far too dangerous for both of them.

Now that his attempt to keep tabs on her had failed, he couldn't help worrying about her.

Which was another entirely new feeling.

Tomorrow he'd run a background check on Faith. If her story panned out, which he expected it would, then he'd set up their next meeting. In the meantime, he'd work on getting access to more of Kerberos's data so he could search for her brother.

Because when they did meet again, Mark fully intended to have news for her. Without it, he knew Faith's wariness would cause her to bolt.

And he didn't plan on losing her.

CHAPTER FOUR

Three Days Later
On the Outskirts of Baltimore

FAITH WASN'T WAITING for him outside the café. She wasn't inside, either. Mark frowned and checked his watch. Yes, he was punctual as usual. Since it was only five minutes past their agreed upon time, it was unreasonable to feel anxious that she wasn't here.

Yet this had been a difficult week with Jamieson, and Mark was impatient to see Faith. To feel the rush of being alive and being somehow better than he knew himself to be.

He wanted to forget what he'd learned this week about Kerberos. Forget that Jamieson was drawing Mark further and further into the clandestine, illegal side of the organization. Letting him learn more about Kaufmann and his diabolical lab.

The information turned Mark's stomach. Normally he hated to show emotion in front of others, but he couldn't control his reaction to the tormented, bestial men that had once been proud soldiers and law enforcement officers. Since Jamieson seemed to take great pleasure in forcing Mark to have more involvement with the lab despite his reservations, he didn't even bother hiding his revulsion. In their current game of power and intimidation, appearing weak made Jamieson trust Mark more.

Mark knew better than to assume that weakness in those around him equaled a lack of threat, but Jamieson apparently believed that as long as he was the strongest man in the game, everyone else could be manipulated to do what he wanted.

The man might have been ruthless enough to move up in rank within the CIA and cunning enough to create an illegal black ops group operating right under the collective noses of the intelligence community, but Mark marveled at how little Jamieson understood human psychology. He fingered the bronze, Etruscan horse in his pocket. It wasn't the original good luck charm that had been in his father's pocket the day he died. No, that one sat on Jamieson's desk. Left out in the open for Mark to see on his last visit to his boss's office.

Another move in the mind games between them. But Mark wasn't going to lose this game. He'd thought he'd killed the man who ordered that his father be tortured to death, but now he knew that he'd been played from the very beginning. Jamieson's possession of the horse was all the proof Mark needed to peg Jamieson as the true mastermind behind his father's death. So he'd do whatever necessary in order to earn Jamieson's trust and gain access to Kerberos's secrets.

Once he possessed sufficient information to guarantee Jamieson would be arrested and his deadly organization shut down, then Mark would contact Ryker, the director of the privately run special operations group, the Surgical Strike Unit. Not too long ago, Mark had been ordered by Jamieson to discredit the SSU, in hopes of driving the organization out of business. Now the SSU had been tasked with finding and stopping those responsible for the missing service personnel and they'd become Mark's ace in the hole for destroying Jamieson.

He gave the café another visual search. Still no Faith. Had Jamieson somehow discovered that she'd followed him to the restaurant the other night and already eliminated her? Or sent her to Kaufmann?

That possibility sent icy tendrils slithering down Mark's spine.

Although everything he knew so far about Dr. Kaufmann's program indicated that the scientist had no interest in experimenting on women, Mark wouldn't put it past Jamieson to send a female to Kaufmann with instructions to let his men use her as they liked.

Mark's fingers curled into fists. That would never happen to Faith. Not if he could help it.

He mentally shook his head. Sometime in the past few days he'd given up trying to understand why Faith mattered so much. Instead, there was a certain thrill to just letting the feeling take control.

He searched the street again. Dammit, where was she?

Had Jamieson found her? Or had she decided not to trust him after all?

But no, there she was, just stepping through the door. Despite the short black bob and light gray eyes, Mark recognized Faith instantly. Their eyes met and Mark forgot all about Jamieson and Kerberos, drowning in the warmth of her gaze. When a customer moved between them, breaking their connection, Mark stifled his annoyance and stepped to the side. He watched Faith weave between people, her head up and her focus on him. Then, as she passed the end of the counter, she glanced over at the large screen television.

Mark lost sight of her again when a couple of men in cheap suits walked into his line of sight. After the men moved away, he saw that Faith's attention was riveted on the screen. Her stricken expression made his gut clench.

He'd almost reached her when she glanced up. Fear, then

fury passed across her beautiful face before she darted into the middle of a family with two strollers containing squealing young children.

What the hell?

Mark craned his neck to see the television. A picture of a house on fire filled the screen. Oh, no. Faith's reaction could only mean one thing. Damn Jamieson's guards. One of them must have spotted Faith with him and been able to make an identification by facial recognition software.

He did his best to hurry after Faith, but the stroller group kept getting in his way. By the time he reached the sidewalk, all he saw of Faith was a flash of her black wig and the bright yellow of her dress as she darted down the street.

Shit. If she turned the corner he'd lose her. He burst into a run, something he never did in public. But this desperation driving him was entirely personal, and for once he didn't care if he drew attention to himself as long as he caught up to Faith.

Luckily for him, a dog tied outside a shop decided that Faith looked like its new best friend and leapt into her path, barking happily and wagging its tail. The few seconds it took for Faith to give the mutt a reluctant pat then dodge around it allowed Mark to catch up to her.

"Faith!" He reached out and grabbed her arm.

She spun and took a swing at him with her fist. Mark easily avoided her blow and captured her wrist with his hand.

"Let go of me," she snarled, "or I swear to God, I'm going to start screaming for the police, you lying bastard."

"What is *wrong* with you?" he snapped.

Faith jerked against his hold. When he didn't loosen his grip, she opened her mouth. Before she could scream, Mark placed his other hand over her lips. "Was that your house burning on the news?"

She blinked at him in surprise, then narrowed her eyes and struck at him.

Mark dropped his hand from her mouth and once again shifted to evade her blow.

"Of course that was my house, you jerk. You ordered the fire!"

With a hiss of annoyance, Mark twisted her arm, turned her away from him, and propelled her forward. "Don't be ridiculous. I didn't have any idea you'd been identified by Jamieson's men until you freaked out back there." Mark hustled Faith toward an alley that led to the back parking lot.

"Give me one good reason why I should believe you," she snarled, struggling to break free.

"I'm not a thug. Give me some credit for being more subtle if I need to intimidate someone."

She glanced at him askew, but at least she stopped fighting him. "That's supposed to reassure me? I should trust you because you're too arrogant to stoop to burning down my house?"

"Yes. Besides, why would I bother to burn down your house? You aren't even staying there, and you don't strike me as the type of person who'd leave her research behind. If I wanted to make sure your notes were obliterated, I'd question you until I was certain I knew all the places you'd hid copies and had discovered the names of everyone you'd talked to about the data. Then I'd eliminate you, your contacts, and the notes."

Her eyes widened and she tugged against his hold on her arm. "So I should be grateful to you because you haven't killed me yet?" The laugh that burst from her throat nudged at the door of hysteria.

A gust of wind blew her hair across her face and she spat it out of her mouth.

For some infernal reason, Mark found the action incredibly erotic. "Woman, you're driving me crazy."

Pulling Faith into the shadow between a dumpster and a large shade tree, Mark spun Faith around so that she faced him and was also out of view of anyone who might step out the back door of the retail building.

She glared up at him, fury and grief swirling in her eyes. "I hate you. I thought you were going to help me. Instead, you sold me out. I've gone for more than a week without any trouble. Then I meet you and the next thing I know, my house burns down. You're a—"

Mark silenced her with a kiss. It started off hard, but quickly softened as the taste of her went straight to his head. His mouth lingered, savoring the softness of her lips as her angry retort melted into a groan of need. As soon as she sighed and relaxed against him, Mark pulled back.

He cradled her head between his hands. "I swear to you, Faith, I didn't betray you. I haven't told anyone that we met."

"You put a damn tracking device in my pocket."

Mark sighed. "To protect you. I wanted to make certain that no one followed you to wherever you were staying."

She crossed her arms over her chest. "No one but you, that is."

For the first time in his life, Mark's intellect was playing a tug-of-war with fiercely protective instincts he hadn't even known he possessed. It made him want to grab Faith and shake some sense into her until she believed him. "I just want you safe, dammit."

"Then tell me, who figured out my identity? I haven't even been home in nine days, so no one followed me there. You can't tell me that my house burned down by accident. Either someone hoped the fire would destroy all my notes, and maybe kill me, too, or the fire was meant as a warning." She shivered. "I'm used to being a target, but a house fire has the potential to spread, particularly in a neighborhood like mine where the houses are close together. What if my neighbors had been hurt?"

Mark gathered her against his chest until he could rest his

chin on the top of her head. His violent need to exact revenge on her behalf shocked him. The fact that she actually let him comfort her filled him with an unfamiliar glow.

"When I saw the house burning on the news, I thought maybe one of the guards had snapped a photo of you and identified you using facial recognition software," he told her. "But on second thought, given that you were already in the car and it was dark, I don't think that's it. Besides," he stroked his hand over her hair. "You were wearing a different wig the other night."

He sighed. "I hope some day you'll trust me enough to reveal the real you."

Faith ignored his comment. "So, if Jamieson's guards didn't discover my identity, and you didn't tell anyone, who burned down my home?"

Mark checked their surroundings. Across the parking lot a trio of young men piled into a Jeep, laughing and punching each other on the shoulder. No one else was in sight. Still, "Not here. Come home with me and we can talk this out. Or let me take you to the safe house. But we need to get someplace where we can't be observed or overheard."

Faith stepped away from him. Her eyes searched his face. For the first time since he'd been a small child, Mark let his expression show all the crazy emotions she stirred in him.

"Please, Faith. Let me keep you safe. Let me help you."

After several agonizing minutes, she nodded. "Okay."

THIS MIGHT JUST BE the dumbest thing she'd ever done, Faith thought as she let herself into her room at the budget hotel chain. After taking a number of evasive actions to get here, including switching vehicles, Mark had reluctantly agreed to stay in the car while she fetched her things. What he didn't realize was that every day she uploaded her notes to a secure server and also mailed copies of them to a postal holding service that had an account shared by her and Toby. There was very little she'd be taking with her that Mark could use against her, if she'd made a mistake and he couldn't be trusted.

But that was the whole issue. She did trust him. Lashing out at him had been her way of dealing with the fear, grief, and sheer fury of seeing her house burning on the news. Now that she had time to think about it, the fire more likely had been set by whoever held Toby.

Faith shuddered. She hated to think of her brother being tortured, and knew that his training would help him hold out a very long time, but it wasn't impossible to think that he'd eventually reveal that he'd sent his notes to Faith. What better first step toward destroying the evidence than burning down her house?

Too bad for them she'd already been on the run.

She pursed her lips. In that case, why hadn't they done the same thing to Toby's place? True, he lived in a high-rise apartment complex with top notch security. Still, even the best security would eventually fall to a determined assailant. So, was it possible that they'd only gone after Faith's home to send her a message? Or had they already tossed Toby's place and discovered that he really didn't keep any notes at home?

She'd have to check the police reports for Toby's neighborhood to see if there was any mention of his apartment being broken into or otherwise damaged. Not that he was around to report a break-in, but maybe a neighbor had noticed something odd.

Faith shoved her few toiletries into her backpack, then used one of her burner phones to access her secure voicemail box, relieved when a message confirmed that Siobahn had checked in on time.

When she called Siobahn back, the call went straight to voicemail. "Hi, Mom. It's me," she said, using their code phrase.

"The weather here in Nassau is beautiful. Wish you were here. Tell Sissy I miss her. Love you. Bye."

Faith told herself she was disappointed to have missed talking to her friend directly, but she knew she lied. She didn't want to have to deal with Siobahn's questions and concern right now.

On her way out of the hotel, she turned off the phone and threw it in the dumpster before returning to Mark.

"Okay," she said as she slipped into the passenger seat. "Where are we going?"

"Safe house." He glanced sideways at her. "Jamieson is monitoring me."

Faith's hand twitched toward the door handle.

"Relax. I've got an anti-bug device in the glove box that will jam any attempt to track us electronically. By the time we get to the safe house no one will be following us and no one will recognize us." He pulled the car out of the parking lot. "The safe house was bought under another identity buried so deep that it would take months for the CIA to tie it back to me."

She gave him a look laden with suspicion. "You were serious before when you said that you have a private safe house?"

Mark smiled. "Absolutely. Spies don't trust anyone. Including, and often particularly, their bosses. We're tools. Valuable only as long as we're useful. Disposable when there's trouble."

Faith wished she didn't understand. But she'd seen too much cruelty and indifference. Experienced situations where human beings were considered nothing but expendable commodities. She imagined that's how Jamieson, or whoever had kidnapped Toby, viewed both Faith and her brother. "I'm sorry."

Mark shrugged. "It was my choice. I could have followed my stepfather into his import-export business. Instead, I decided I liked the thrill of outmaneuvering other spies who operate in the shadows of the business world."

"Sounds like you have lots of interesting stories to tell." She tilted her head. "Unless they're all classified?"

"I'm certain I can come up with one or two I could share." He glanced at her out of the corner of his eye. "What would I get in return?"

The gleam in his eye let her know exactly what he wanted. "I—" Her stomach gurgled loudly. She felt her cheeks heat. "Sorry."

Mark laughed softly. "Don't apologize. We can grab lunch before we hit the safe house."

AFTER ENOUGH EVASIVE action to satisfy even Faith's paranoia, they ended up sharing fried chicken and biscuits at a picnic table in a deserted corner of a beachside park. The look of faint disdain on Mark's face as he ate the meal almost made Faith laugh, but she knew he'd take it the wrong way. He was just so cute when he got all fussy and arrogant. But eating at an upscale restaurant would have been out of character for their worn jeans and threadbare t-shirts. Mark even wore a ragged army jacket that made him look dangerously sexy.

Although, from the look on his face, Mark didn't approve of their apparel any more than he did their food. And if the way he'd carefully brushed off the picnic table and bench was any indication, he wasn't a fan of eating outdoors. While she found his fastidiousness odd—with his training he had to have slummed it from time to time on a mission—she felt a warm glow in the vicinity of her heart knowing that he was willing to ignore his distaste in order to help keep her safe.

"So," she said after she'd devoured several pieces of chicken and two biscuits, "I finally cracked the code on the remaining file on Toby's flash drive. There wasn't much new there, except he quoted several sources as claiming that some of Kerberos's special teams were going to help out the President on an unspecified mission."

Mark's hand froze on the way to his mouth, then he set down the piece of chicken he'd been about to eat.

"That means something to you," Faith said.

"Maybe."

"What—"

"No, Faith. I can't tell you."

The chill in his voice raised her hackles. As she opened her mouth to protest, he shook his head. "All I have now are a few vague rumors. Are you certain there were no specifics in Toby's notes?"

She nodded.

"Okay. I'll have to look into this. If I find out anything concrete, I'll let you know."

Faith knew she'd have to settle for that. "So, what do you have for me on Toby's disappearance?"

Mark cleaned his greasy fingers with a wet wipe before answering. "I haven't found any mention of your brother yet. But Jamieson has assigned me to search lists of military and law enforcement personnel and identify potential candidates for the enhanced soldier program."

"Did you…" Faith forced herself not to scoot away as alarm flashed through her. "Did you actually pick men out to be kidnapped?"

He sighed. Neatly stacked his lunch debris in a small pile before answering. "Yes."

Oh, God. Had she been wrong about him?

She started to push to her feet, but Mark tugged gently on her wrist. "Sit down, Faith. It's not as bad as it seems. Yes, I provided names of potential candidates to Jamieson. But as I mentioned before, I'm working against him. I also gave the data to a privately run special operations group called the Surgical

Strike Unit. The SSU's goal is to shut the scientific program down. They'll make certain no harm comes to the men."

Some of the tension drained out of her, leaving her shaky.

"Just how much do you know about the program, Faith?"

She shrugged. "Basically what I told you before. Toby's notes make it clear that the aim of the program is to create superhuman soldiers, but he never explains what that means. Only that the subjects appear to end up with bulkier bodies and to suffer from insane rages."

"Okay." He nodded, as if coming to a decision. "What I'm about to tell you has to stay between us, Faith. No future articles by you or any of your contacts. Promise?"

"No."

His mouth thinned. "Then—"

She raised her hand in a stopping gesture. "Hold your horses, mister. I'm not done. I promise not to share what you're about to tell me unless I think the information needs to be released in order to save Toby's life or the life of anyone else. I also can't promise that my colleagues won't eventually manage to ferret out the information on their own." She'd lay odds that Siobahn would manage to find the truth if she dug hard enough.

Mark's shoulders lowered and he nodded. "Okay, that's fair."

Suspecting that it was hard for him to confide in anyone, let alone a near stranger, Faith squeezed his hand.

He responded with a faint smile. "I'll try to make this as short as possible. For several years the Department of Defense and the CIA jointly supported a lab with the goal of creating men with enhanced skills that would better suit their mission objectives. Increased strength for the DOD. More speed and improved mental abilities for the CIA. Little need for sleep. An inability to feel pain."

"But...how?"

"I'm not sure of the details, but my understanding is that the scientists used a combination of steroids and other drugs, including custom-created chemicals. There may also have been hypnosis, gene manipulation, and torture. They wanted a soldier who could carry out his mission without stopping to sleep or eat, and who was so focused on the objective that only his death would stop him."

"That sounds like something out of a science fiction movie!"

"It gets worse. The scientists found a way to alter their subjects' brains and make them susceptible to mind control."

Faith shivered. Had anyone else been telling her this, she'd have brushed them off as delusional or too easily fooled. But Mark seemed too coldly pragmatic to believe in wild speculation. And hadn't Toby's note mentioned he might be turned into a creature that would kill her on their order? At the time, Faith hadn't known what he meant, so she'd dismissed it as hype. Now, though, she was beginning to understand.

Mark pushed his lunch debris into a tighter pile, then brushed a few crumbs off the tabletop. "The head scientist at the lab, Dr. Mikhail Nevsky, was close to achieving his objectives, but there were deadly side effects. Insanity. Uncontrollable rage. Massive organ shutdown. Before he could perfect his program, Nevsky died in a fire that consumed his lab. However, he'd saved copies of his notes on a microchip."

He turned his head to look at her. "Word got out about the existence of the chip. Every criminal and governmental organization wanted the microchip—most particularly the military and the intelligence agencies. Jamieson ordered me to find the chip and bring it to him before he'd give me the name of the man who killed my father. That offer was, of course, made before I discovered that Jamieson was the one responsible for my father's death." His expression hardened. "I countered with a demand that in exchange for the chip, he also let me into Kerberos."

Faith sucked in a breath.

"Back then," Mark continued, "I approved of what I knew of the organization's mission. Kerberos's goal is to strike at our country's enemies in the most effective way possible, without regard to the law. I've seen too much damage done by short-sighted politicians to want to be shackled by their lack of courage. So I joined the hunt for the microchip."

Mark tapped his fingers against the table. "However, it turned out that Nevsky's right-hand man, a scientist named Dr. Leonard Kaufmann, had survived the fire and started his own lab. Funded, as your brother discovered, by Jamieson and Kerberos." Mark laced his fingers through hers. "Faith, if Jamieson ordered Toby kidnapped and sent over to Kaufmann's lab, you have to understand what this means. The men in the program don't just become susceptible to mind control. They lose their ability to think at more than a basic level."

She yanked her hand away and stood up. "What are you saying?"

"One of the SSU's agents, Rafe Andros, was recently captured during a mission to investigate Kaufmann's lab. By the time the SSU rescued him, Andros could only communicate in grunts and monosyllables, because the drugs he'd been given blocked his intelligence. He acted like a rabid animal—snapping and lashing out at everyone who came near him. Faith, he tried to kill his own brother. Apparently they brainwashed him into thinking all his family members and close friends were enemies who needed to be destroyed."

Faith shook her head and moved away from the picnic table, nearly blinded by panic. She'd suspected that Toby had been conscripted into the program, but she'd assumed that the effects would be something he could fight against. That the insanity and rages would stop once the harmful drugs were out of his system.

Now Mark wanted her to believe that her sharp, witty

brother would end up no better than some dumb beast, under the influence of mind control that would make him try to kill his own sister.

"No!"

Faith turned and raced toward the water. "NO!" she shouted to the sky. "I refuse to believe it. Do you hear me?" She'd lost her parents, her sister, her career and now her home. She needed to believe that whatever happened to Toby could be reversed. "You will not destroy my brother. You. Will. Not!"

But the pressure inside her chest said that fate could, and would hurt Toby, because Faith's wishes didn't matter. Unable to stand the thought, she sprinted down the beach, ignoring Mark's shouts behind her.

She couldn't bear another loss. She just couldn't. She wasn't strong enough.

So she ran.

CHAPTER FIVE

MARK CURSED himself for an insensitive lout as he watched Faith sprint down the beach. He should have thought more carefully about whether to reveal the side effects of Kaufmann's program. But he'd been so blindsided by the new experience of trusting another person enough to confide in them, that he'd failed to consider that a caring woman like Faith wouldn't want to know that her brother might be programmed to kill her.

Keeping an eye on Faith, Mark gathered the debris from their lunch and tossed it in a trashcan. Then he headed down the beach toward her. At least he hadn't gone into specifics about the program. He hadn't told her what he'd witnessed in Ivanov's lab and the strange effect seeing those men had had on his conscience.

Even worse, he'd just received confirmation that Kaufmann indeed had an accelerated program in place. Normally, a subject would take many weeks to transition into the optimal level required for inclusion on a Kerberos team. But if his latest information was correct, the accelerated program required only two weeks.

Which meant that Toby might not have the time they needed to save him.

For perhaps the first time since his mother and stepfather died, Mark cared about another person's feelings. He hated knowing that Faith was hurting over Toby's situation.

Up ahead, Faith dropped to her knees. Her head and shoulders curled forward and it looked like she'd buried her fists in the sand.

Mark slowed as he approached her. "Faith."

She exploded up out of her crouch. Sand sailed toward his head and he realized she'd thrown it at him. "You've known this was a likely scenario since I met you and yet you said nothing. You let me... Let me..."

Mark grabbed her hands as they aimed for his face. "You said you suspected that Toby had been captured and put into the program. How was I supposed to know that you had no clue what that meant? If I'd realized your ignorance, I would have saved you this emotional pain." He took a deep breath. "Don't lose hope. Not yet. I can't prove Jamieson had anything to do with your brother's disappearance. Toby might have been killed in an accident someplace so remote that his body hasn't been found yet. He might have been captured or killed by enemies he made while conducting another investigation."

Faith's tear-stained, grief-ravaged face tore something loose inside of him. Mark couldn't stand it any more. He pulled her against his chest and held her as she cried.

"I'm sorry," she sobbed, clutching hold of Mark's shirt. "I knew it was possible he'd been changed. Just not to the extent that you mentioned. I can't...I can't bear the idea that he might be trapped inside his mind, forced to act against his beliefs."

Mark's chin settled on the top of her head. "I can't promise you that you'll get back the brother you once knew," he said. "But I will promise that I'll do everything possible to find him."

Her arms tightened around him. "Please. He's my only remaining family. I can't lose him. I just can't."

"I understand. After my father died, I didn't want to be out of sight of my mother."

Faith pushed away from him and swiped her hand over her face to dry her tears. "How old were you?"

Mark shook his head. "Not here." Glancing around, he guided Faith toward a patch of sand sheltered by a fall of rocks. He removed his jacket and laid it down, then sat with his back against the rocks and Faith cradled against his chest. A remote part of his brain marveled at how he'd lowered himself to the sand without protest, when a few months ago he would have turned up his nose at sitting on anything less than a beach chair on top of a blanket. But the newly awakened part of him enjoyed putting Faith's comfort first.

Once they were settled, he asked, "So, what do you want to know?"

IF FAITH'S life got any weirder, she'd start to wonder if she'd been cast in a movie without realizing it. In the space of an hour she'd ricocheted from fury and grief over seeing her house burn, to agonizing fear upon realizing Toby might be forever altered, to this aching tenderness over the gentle way Mark was treating her. The man might be a cold hearted bastard in his job, but he'd been nothing but considerate with her.

"Tell me about your family," she finally said. "Did Jamieson truly order your father killed? Is that really why you're working against him?"

Mark exhaled loudly. His cheek pressed against hers as he stared at the waves crashing against the shore. "It's...complicated. The short answer is yes. And no."

Faith laced her fingers with his and crossed both their arms over her middle. Then she turned her head and placed a soft kiss on his jaw.

Mark's lips lifted into a half-smile. "My father was a judge in Boston, but his father was from Sicily. Part of the mafioso before he immigrated to America. My father was proud that he'd broken family tradition and was clean his entire life. He taught me not only to obey the law, but to love and respect it."

He tightened his clasp on her fingers. "But when I was five, my father was kidnapped, tortured, and then dumped on our front lawn." Mark cleared his throat and Faith braced herself. "He died in my arms."

Faith pressed a kiss to his cheek. "Mark, I'm so sorry."

"Everyone assumed it was retaliation for my father's work, but no one was ever arrested for the crime."

Faith heard the pain of the little boy in Mark's voice and snuggled closer to him, drawing soothing circles on the backs of his hands with her thumbs.

"My mother was Russian and had never really fit into Boston society. She wanted to be with her family again, so three years later, we moved to Moscow. At first, all was well. We lived in relative comfort. Then the patriarch of the family died and his successor didn't get along with my mother. Later, I learned that under his guidance, one of Mother's cousins had taken control of the money that came from her widow benefits and my father's life insurance policy. He used the money to try and recoup the family's losses from bad investments. Instead, he lost Mother's money, too. But at the time, all I knew was that there was a huge fight and they threw us out. Mother and I ended up in a substandard apartment in the poorest section of town, barely able to afford the rent from the meager funds she had left.

"Because she'd been raised in high society, and my father's job had ensured that she didn't have to work, my mother didn't have any marketable skills. She couldn't find a job and we soon ran out of money. I went out onto the streets and quickly learned how to beg or steal enough so that we could buy food and keep up with the rent."

Faith bit her lip to keep back her cry of protest.

"I didn't care who I hurt or wronged, as long as my mother had food and shelter. Every lesson my father had taught me went down the drain. Survival was everything."

"How long were you on the streets?"

He shrugged. "On and off for about three years."

This time she couldn't keep her mouth shut. "Oh, Mark!"

"It wasn't so bad. I soon earned a reputation. The other kids were afraid of me and that afforded me some protection."

"Didn't your mother worry about you? Wasn't there anyone in your family who could have helped you?"

"I didn't realize it at the time, but my mother was severely depressed. Her focus was turned so completely inward that..." He coughed, then fell silent.

"What?"

"I'm not sure she always remembered that she had a son."

Her throat too tight to speak, Faith repositioned herself so that she sat inside the protection of Mark's arm, with her head on his shoulder. Then she pressed a kiss over his heart, moved deeply by the trust he showed by revealing his childhood to her. Now she understood why he'd developed such a callous attitude. Why he didn't think of the potential pain his actions caused others. Mark's emotional scars, whether or not he admitted to them, ran deep.

She also understood why he was so fastidious. It was a reaction to the time he'd spent on the streets. She could picture him as a grubby boy in threadbare clothes, scowling fiercely as he fought to earn enough money to keep him and his mother alive.

"My mother eventually came out of her grieving period and took more responsibility for her life," Mark said. "She managed to land a job as a hostess in a tea house, but she barely made enough to pay for food and our room. However, she enrolled me in school, which I hated. I didn't want to leave her." He hesitated.

"You were afraid that you'd come home and find out that something had happened to her?"

"Yes." Mark took a deep breath. "But she insisted, so I went to school. Then, a few months later, she met my stepfather."

At the affection she heard in Mark's voice, the hard, tight knot in Faith's chest unwound.

"Talk about a fairytale romance. Sergei was a millionaire who owned an import-export business. He met my mother when he took a client to tea in the place where she worked. According to him, it was love at first sight. Before I knew it, they were married and the three of us were living in his palatial apartment. He even launched an investigation into the theft of Mother's money, and eventually won back some of her funds."

Faith smiled at the way he said the words with such fierce satisfaction.

"My stepfather took me under his wing. Trained me to succeed in business. He pointed out that the tricks I'd developed in order to survive on the street could be used to read and manipulate people in business deals. He taught me who was important to know and who it was mandatory to please. Most of all, he told me that it was possible to be a successful businessman—even in Moscow—and adhere to a code of honor."

Mark's fingers teased at the edges of Faith's black wig and she wished she could rip the damn thing off and show him the real her. But she had to be smarter than that. Even here on this isolated section of beach she feared detection.

"I didn't always listen to my stepfather," Mark continued. "Trusting people didn't come easily to me. I still considered myself in a fight for survival. Particularly once I was shipped off to boarding school, where I was picked on for being an

American, even though by then I'd lived almost a third of my life in Russia. Still, I worked hard and rose to the top of my class. All the while studying my fellow students for behaviors I could mimic or weaknesses I could exploit in order to increase my status."

Faith shook her head, her cheek rubbing against his chest. "I bet the other kids were scared of you. A badass straight off the streets. Did you bloody a lot of noses?"

Mark gave what she was coming to realize was an uncharacteristic snort. "Perhaps a few." The satisfaction in his tone spoke to the tally being much more than a few. "I did have a lot of catching up to do, having missed so many years of school. But I eventually achieved parity with my peers. And my experience there is what led me to seek employment with the CIA."

"How so? I can't imagine the CIA recruiting in Russian boarding schools."

Mark shifted position, so that Faith fit more snugly against him. "You're right. It was nothing so direct as that. I didn't get approached by the CIA until I was back in the United States, majoring in business at Harvard. But while reading *Crime and Punishment* in high school, I became obsessed with the idea of finding and killing the men who'd kidnapped and tortured my father to death. To do that, I needed strength. Skills. Power."

"Men? But I thought you said Jamieson ordered the hit?"

Mark's hand clenched in her hair, then relaxed. "As I mentioned, the initial conclusion everyone made was that the hit had been ordered by a mob boss in retaliation for a unfavorable verdict handed down by my father. However, no one was ever arrested for the murder. After I'd been with the CIA for several years, I uncovered the names of those responsible for kidnapping and torturing my father, and I...uh..."

"You killed them, didn't you?"

Mark's body tensed underneath her. The silence stretched out. Finally, he said, "Yes. That's the kind of man I am, Faith."

She ran her hand lightly down his chest. "That's okay. I... I've been to that mental place where I was so angry and so hurt that I contemplated murder. But I still don't see the connection to Jamieson."

"I always assumed that the mobsters I killed were the only ones involved. Then Jamieson told me he had proof that the man who'd hired the mobsters to torture and kill my father was still alive. Bringing him Nevsky's microchip became the price for that information. And for my admission into Kerberos."

"So...you gave him the microchip?"

Mark's chest rose under her cheek. "No. It turned out that Nevsky had a daughter that no one knew about. He arranged to have the microchip implanted in her abdomen during an appendectomy. The chip then received updates via a high powered radio receiver."

Faith flinched. "Oh. My. God. His daughter agreed to this?"

"No. She didn't even know her father. Her mother had run from Dr. Nevsky when their daughter was still an infant. Unfortunately, we learned that the microchip was booby-trapped. Anyone who tried to remove it without knowing how to disable the trap would release a poison that would kill the woman."

Faith craned her neck to peer up at him, her stomach dropping. There was something in his voice. "Were you in love with her?"

Mark's body tensed. "I...um..." He swallowed heavily, but she had to give him credit. He met her eyes. "I thought I was."

Faith bit her lip and glanced away, but he put his finger under her chin and turned her face so she was forced to meet his gaze. "Faith, what I felt for Susana Dias—"

She shoved away from him. "Susana Dias the supermodel? The woman who now has her own show on the Adventure Channel that documents her archaeological digs? That's Dr. Nevsky's daughter?" No wonder Mark had fallen in love with her. The woman possessed a sultry Brazilian beauty, had a love for life that shone fiercely from her eyes, and was intelligent to boot.

Mark grabbed her shoulders. "Faith, listen to me. Yes, I was dazzled by Susana Dias. Looking back, though, what I felt for her was infatuation. The need to prove myself a better man by impressing such a celebrity. But it wasn't real. *This* is real." He bent his head and kissed her with a hunger Faith was helpless to deny.

When they came up for air, she murmured, "So what happened?"

His mouth flattened and he pulled Faith against his chest, blocking her view of his expression. "I kidnapped Susana Dias and took her to Moscow to the lab of one of Dr. Nevsky's colleagues. Dr. Ivanov was the only man capable of safely removing the microchip. However, an SSU agent named Kai Paterson followed us to Moscow. There was a fight in Ivanov's lab, and Paterson swallowed the microchip to prevent Ivanov from taking it. So I gave Jamieson a dummy microchip, then pretended innocence when the data on the chip turned out to be nonsense. That's one of the reasons Jamieson doesn't fully trust me. He doesn't know if I made an honest mistake with the chip or deliberately acted against him."

He sighed. "During a meeting in Jamieson's office a week ago, I noticed on his desk a small, bronze, Etruscan horse with a dent in its shoulder. It was my father's good luck piece that had been missing from his pockets when he died. I'd searched all over for the horse, wanting it as a memento of my father. When I spotted it next to Jamieson's desk telephone, I knew then that he'd been playing me all along. Jamieson was the one who'd ordered my father's death."

Faith's heart ached for the little boy needing something to hold onto as a keepsake from his father. "But why let you see the horse?"

"It's just another move in the mind games we're playing with one another."

Faith sat up so she could stare at Mark. "You're walking a dangerous line. I don't want you taking any unnecessary risks to help me."

Mark planted a hard kiss on her mouth. "I started down this road before I met you, Faith. Looking for evidence of what happened to your brother isn't going to increase the likelihood that Jamieson will figure out what I'm up to."

"But—"

Another kiss. "Do you have any idea how touched I am that you care?"

Damn him. There he went again, melting her heart.

"But I'm an experienced agent, Faith. Don't give up on me. Together, we'll bring down Jamieson."

She gave a rueful smile. "Together. I like the sound of that."

"That's the best you could think of? To burn down the sister's house?" Wayne Jamieson let his disdain seep into his voice and tightened his grip on the phone. He was going to have to speak with Dr. Kaufmann again about inflating his reports regarding the abilities of the men he sent to Kerberos. This supposed assassin from the new, intelligence boosting side of Kaufmann's program possessed minimal creativity and displayed a distinct lack of ability to predict possible outcomes from his actions. "Did it occur to you to set a trap for her instead? Question her friends and neighbors by force to find out where the woman has disappeared to? Did you even search her house before you set it on fire?"

"Yes, sir. I searched her house. There was nothing helpful. Questioning her acquaintances does not fall within my orders."

Jamieson caught the eye of the Mona Lisa staring at him from the print that hung to the left of his desk. Her expression assured him that she sympathized with his frustration. He tapped the blotter of his desk with the end of his pen. "Very well. You are relieved of duty. Report back to your handler."

Using extreme care, Jamieson replaced the handset on its cradle. It wouldn't do to let his temper show in a physical way. With the upcoming anniversary demonstration for the President, plus the investigation by the SSU, Jamieson had to assume he was under constant surveillance. Yes, his office had electronic jamming technology in place, but if he became accustomed to letting his emotions show here, he might slip some day when he wasn't alone. And if there was one thing he prided himself on, it was on always maintaining his calm demeanor.

He pressed the intercom button to summon his secretary. "Mrs. Perry, please bring me the Andrews file."

The team that had captured Toby Andrews had been one of Jamieson's newest squads of unaltered Kerberos soldiers. His preference would have been to keep those men in charge of monitoring the DOD's investigation into Andrews's disappearance and to deal with the sister, who according to the information extracted during torture, now held all of Andrews's research into Kerberos and Kaufmann's program.

But the President had demanded some pre-attack reconnaissance and other preparation work that required both intelligence and strength. With the rest of his normal teams otherwise occupied, Jamieson had split this last team up and assigned each of them to work with a group of altered soldiers in order to fulfill the President's assignments. Leaving only the still untested, intelligence enhanced soldiers to stall the DOD and SSU's investigations and to track down Faith Andrews.

Kerberos analysts were still searching through hours of video from security cameras, trying to locate the Andrews woman. It was a slow, labor intensive process, even using facial recognition software. So far, the woman hadn't been spotted on tape.

Their inability to discover her whereabouts puzzled him. For pity's sake, the woman taught college and high school students. It wasn't as if she were an experienced spy. So why couldn't anyone find her?

CHAPTER SIX

"Siobahn, I'm fine, really," Faith said when she called her friend the next day. "I'm more concerned about you. You've got to stop your investigation. These people are serious about keeping their secrets." She was used to physical and psychological intimidation from her overseas assignments. But suspecting that people within her own government might have burned down her house made it clear how much danger she'd put her friend in. She'd confirmed with a police contact that someone had trashed Toby's apartment, but she had no idea how long ago that had occurred. Probably before he'd been kidnapped and he told them that he didn't keep his notes at home. Still, she didn't want Siobahn becoming a victim to a similar crime.

Don't leave the safe house.

Mark had given her that warning just before he'd left for work this morning. Odd, how much she missed him, when for the past ten days she'd had no contact with her friends and colleagues except for her phone calls and emails to Siobahn. Faith had wanted to warn her friend today, but hadn't felt comfortable holding the conversation in Mark's safe house. She might have temporarily decided to trust him regarding her own safety, but she wasn't going to trust Siobahn's life to him.

While she appreciated Mark's concern, she refused to be kept prisoner. So she'd donned another disguise, then taken a bus to retrieve her car, before driving to this deserted public park.

"No, Faith, you listen. Your house burned down. You know as well as I do that means you're close to the truth. They were trying to scare you."

"Or destroy my notes."

"Right. Like any smart reporter keeps only one copy of her notes."

Faith had to agree with Siobahn on that one. "So, we agree the fire was a message." The news reports had flashed Faith's photo, mentioned that authorities had been unable to locate her, and told the public to call with any information.

Faith felt guilty about not letting her friends and coworkers know she was safe, but she didn't dare contact them.

Unfortunately, having a helpful public looking for her only made it crucial that she keep wearing disguises. While the selection of wigs and clothing she'd pulled from Toby's cabin had been extensive—they'd made it a fun project to add items to the stockpile on a regular basis—she was at the point where she'd need to stop by a thrift shop to add clothes so she didn't achieve the same look twice.

"Of course, the fire isn't going to stop my investigation," Faith said. "Not that these past few days have been very productive. I've asked my few contacts within the military and law enforcement communities for help, but either they have nothing to add or they won't talk to me."

"Same here."

"Just another reason for you to bow out Siobahn. You've done what you can. Now let me finish it." Hopefully, Mark would be able to locate Toby soon. Then Faith would bring him home, no matter what shape he was in. "I won't be able to live with myself if you end up hurt."

"Faith, you know I never let go of a story," Siobahn chided.

"Please, Siobahn. You need to drop this one. I've made a new contact who has inside information and I'm confident that we're close to finding Toby. Please don't do anything to stir up the people involved. If Toby has been kidnapped, they might kill him if they think you're too close to exposing them. So I'm begging you to let this go. Just for now. I promise that I'll update you once Toby is safe."

"But will I be able to print what you tell me?"

"No. You know as well as I do that this program is highly classified. You'll never get the verification you need in order to go to print."

"Dammit, Faith."

"I know." She understood the frustration in her friend's voice. Faith also hated the idea of keeping this level of treachery quiet. "But if my contact is correct, the men involved will be brought to justice." She gave a rough laugh. "Honestly though? All I care about right now is saving my brother."

Siobahn sighed. "Fine. I'll back off so I won't put your brother in danger. But if there's any way I can get a story out of this, you know I'm going to run with it."

Faith closed her eyes in relief. "I know. Thank you. This is the last time I'm going to contact you directly until it's over. I—"

"Oh no, you don't. You're going to continue to check in with me or I'm going to hunt you down."

Faith laughed. "I'm not sure if I'm lucky or cursed to have such a loyal friend."

"Lucky, of course." Siobahn gave another sigh. "You trust this contact?"

"As much as I trust anyone I've just met." More, actually. Which still worried the cynical side of her.

"All right, then. Contact me on our regular schedule and I'll back off. For now."

Knowing that was as good as she was going to get, Faith nodded even though her friend couldn't see her. "Thanks, Siobahn."

"YOU WERE SUPPOSED to stay at the safe house!" Mark's anger and concern crackled over the phone line.

Faith couldn't help it. She grinned as she walked toward the outdoor patio of the café where she'd arranged to meet Mark. She loved the fact that she could make him lose his arrogant calm. "And I told you, I know how to stay under the radar. In fact, I bet you look right past me when I show up."

Mark snorted and said so softly she almost didn't hear him, "I'd recognize you anywhere."

"Fine. Bet's on. See you soon." She disconnected as she rounded the corner and came within sight of the café. Her foolish grin grew wider as she spotted Mark. His back was to her. Perfect. She tucked her disposable phone into the paper bag containing the remains of the brownie she'd scarfed down with her coffee and tossed it into the nearest trashcan. This afternoon she was dressed like an upscale business woman, with a tight, plum colored suit, a wig with blonde hair done in a neat chignon, and four-inch stilettos that made her feet ache.

She figured this disguise was closest to the type of woman Mark normally dated. Not that she and Mark were dating. And not that he'd said anything about his preferences. Still, he was so fussy that she could only picture him with high-class, polished women.

Which was not Faith at all. She was messy, both literally and emotionally. When in pursuit of a story, she didn't care what she looked like as long as she could move quickly and comfortably. Mark's women probably went through the day constantly checking to make sure that not a hair fell out of place.

Realizing that she was scowling, Faith smoothed her features into a polite mask and prepared to stroll right by Mark.

But as she got within hailing distance, his body stiffened and he turned around. His eyes met hers and flared with recognition. Damn. How'd he do that?

As his gaze warmed, his mouth curled up into one of his rare smiles and he walked toward her, both hands reaching out for hers.

The shot of desire that hit Faith was embarrassing. She considered herself a practical woman. One more likely to lead with her head than her heart and who didn't believe in love at first sight. While she had a healthy libido, she'd never been so overwhelmed by lust that the needs of her body overrode her common sense or her need to get to the truth.

So what was it about Mark that reached inside her and started a fire? Sure, he was attractive in that *GQ* metrosexual way, with his expensive suits and his neatly trimmed dark brown hair. But she'd always been drawn to scruffier men. Indiana Jones instead of James Bond.

Yet there was something about Mark, some hint of the wolf in sheep's clothing that caught her attention. Hell, he'd even admitted that he wasn't a particularly nice guy, yet the confession did nothing to ease the need crawling through her, urging her to get as close to Mark as physically possible.

She gave him a rueful smile and let him take both her hands in his. He held her at arm's length, giving her the once over.

"Like what you see?" she asked.

He gave a slight shake of his head, then moved in to buss her cheeks European style. "No. You look gorgeous, Faith, but this isn't you. I might not have seen your real hair or your true eye color, but I've noticed that you're much more relaxed when wearing those casual, funky clothes than this urban armor."

God. How was she supposed to resist him when he understood her so well? "How'd you know it was me?" she murmured as he hooked his arm through hers.

He glanced over at her. "Instinct."

She rolled her eyes. "Some super spy sixth sense?"

A flush stained his cheeks and he looked away.

"What?" she demanded.

He shrugged. "It's you. Yes, as a spy I have a keen sense for danger. But somehow I've also developed an acute awareness of you."

"You could pick me out blind in a dark room?" she joked.

"Yes." The quiet admission made her heart turn over. He continued to amaze her with statements like this, causing more than just a spike in her libido. These moments of connection, combined with her sheer joy at seeing him, made it clear she was in deep emotional waters. Drowning fast.

She slid her hand down his arm until she could twine her fingers around his, and was relieved when he clasped her hand back. "It's totally nuts, but I feel the same way," she confessed.

"Good." He stopped and pulled her in for a brief kiss. "Let's get you back to the safe house."

Just that brief touch of lips lit her up like a bonfire. "I want you," she murmured.

Heat sparked in his eyes. "Hold that thought." Grabbing her hand again, he hustled her down the street.

What she felt for Mark went far beyond the need to use sex in order to escape the ever growing fear inside her. She'd had short affairs before where the purpose had simply been to bring some sort of balance into her life under circumstances that threatened to break her.

This felt like so much more. While she desperately wanted a physical release, just being with Mark calmed her and lessened her fear that Toby was slipping farther and farther away from her each day.

With each step they took, Faith's arousal grew. *I want you. I want you. I want you.*

She was in way over her head. So consumed by her need to touch Mark that she barely paid any attention as he led her to his car, then drove a convoluted route to the safe house.

She barely let him lock the door behind them and set the exterior alarm before she ran her hands across his shoulders and down his back.

Sleek muscle tensed under his fitted suit jacket. "Off," she murmured.

His body shook with laughter, but when Mark turned around, his eyes held equal parts confusion and lust. "This is crazy. I'm not... I don't..."

She reached up and placed a kiss on his mouth. "I know. I feel like I've been drugged with a powerful aphrodisiac. All I want is to crawl inside you."

His breath caught, then he put his hands behind her head and brought his mouth to hers in a kiss that revealed the uncivilized core of him. His lips plundered. She welcomed every hard thrust of his tongue, pressing her body against him in hopes of relieving some of the tension building inside her.

Her fingers shoved at his suit jacket. Mark let go of her head long enough to shrug off the jacket, then he gripped her head again, his hold just short of painful as he took her mouth.

Panting slightly, he lifted his head and stared at her. His pupils were dilated and a flush darkened his cheeks. She loved seeing the effects of his arousal, and her body responded in kind.

He tugged at her hair. "Wig. Off."

Nodding, Faith helped him remove the elegant coiffure, then arched into his touch as he massaged her scalp. "Mmm."

He combed out her chin length, dark blonde curls with his fingers. "I like it," he murmured.

She knew her hair, fashionably untidy at the best of times, must look a mess after being matted under the wig. But Mark's eyes reflected nothing but desire before he lowered his mouth again to hers.

She sighed in pleasure, sinking into the kiss. But after a minute or so she began to squirm against him. "Need to touch your skin. Now."

Yet it was hard to think what to do next with his mouth making love to hers with such contained violence. Using her nails, she scrabbled at the buttons on his shirt until a few of them gave. She snuck her fingers inside the gap, and met the soft cotton of his undershirt.

She growled in frustration and bit his tongue.

"Hey!" Mark pulled back. "What the hell was that for?"

"Take your shirt off." Not bothering to wait for his compliance, her fingers went to work on his buttons. But there was something wrong. Her normally agile fingers couldn't seem to make sense of the complicated act of pushing the buttons free of their holes.

"Let me." The laughter in Mark's voice made Faith glance up in surprise. She had a feeling he didn't laugh very often. If asked, she'd guess that he usually took sex as seriously as he seemed to take everything else.

"You should laugh more," she said, then winced at the inanity of telling the man she wanted to see naked that she wanted him to laugh at her.

But Mark got it.

He pressed a quick kiss to her mouth. "Only with you." He shook his head. "You make me feel young. Light." Another brief kiss. "Desperate." He gave a self-deprecating smile. "I haven't felt this way in years."

Faith stared at him, dumbfounded. Then he slipped out of

his shirt and pulled his undershirt up over his head and she was left staring dumbly at a beautifully sculpted male chest. "Who knew you hid such perfection under those stuffy shirts?" she blurted.

My God, was that a tinge of red on his cheeks? She'd made super spy Mark Tonelli blush?

"Let's see what you're concealing, Faith." His hands slipped under her short-sleeved, silk blouse and in one swift move lifted it over her head and tossed it aside. "Ah. Beautiful."

Now it was her turn to blush. She wasn't exactly model thin or in as good shape as she'd been when trotting all over the world, either running toward danger in pursuit of a story or running away from those who wanted to stop her from exposing the truth. But the heat in Mark's eyes made her feel sexy all the way to her core. And when he reached out and reverently stroked his finger along the lace edge of her bra over first her left and then her right breast, she shivered.

Reaching behind to unfasten the back clasp of her bra, she shrugged her shoulders so that the straps loosened and the bra fell off in his hand.

"Perfection," Mark whispered. He lowered his head and traced a line of kisses from her throat down to her left nipple. Then he sucked the tight bud into his mouth. Lightning shot to her center and she gasped.

How on earth did he manage to rev her so fast?

Her fists tangled in his hair, pulling him closer. Heat spiraled through her, filling her up until it pressed against her skin and she thought she'd explode if she couldn't relieve the pressure. "Mark! I need you. Now." She tugged at his hair, trying to get him to move up so she could press her hips against him. But his only response was to nip at the sensitive skin of her areola, then move on to the other breast.

"Mark," she whimpered. "You're killing me."

"Good." He finally raised his head and the heat in his eyes

nearly incinerated her. "Because no one has ever driven me so crazy in my life." He took her mouth in a fierce kiss.

Faith finally got her hands around his back, slid them down to cup his buttocks, and pulled him tightly against her. While their mouths dueled, Faith rubbed herself against the hard length pressing against her belly and felt her tension ratchet toward a small orgasm.

"Oh no, you don't," Mark growled. "Not without me." He scooped her into his arms so quickly that she squeaked in alarm and threw her arm around his neck for balance as he strode for the stairs.

"Is there anything sexier than being carried to bed by a gorgeous man," she murmured, kicking her feet for the sheer pleasure of it. Joy bubbled up inside her, as if she'd drunk too much champagne. Another side effect of too much stress. Sometimes the release came in the form of inappropriate humor. Sometimes arousal.

Apparently Mark tapped into both her need for sex and for a lightening of her mood.

"Enjoy it while it lasts," he shot back.

Startled at how his comment mirrored her thoughts, she glanced up at him.

Mark smiled down at her, but there was no acknowledgment in his eyes that he'd understood her train of thought. Just bemusement over his behavior. "I'm not usually the caveman type. In fact, I pride myself on being a considerate, deliberate, civilized lover."

"Oh, baby, I'm so sorry." Faith patted his chest with her free hand. "Sex shouldn't be quiet and polite. It should be noisy and enthusiastic and primal. You've been missing out."

She let her fingers find his nipple and gave it a little pinch.

Mark made a sound that was half surprise and half pleasure. "So teach me, witch."

She raised her brows and gave him a look. "Witch?"

"Of course. Who else but a witch could have enchanted me so thoroughly?"

Faith decided that she liked having put that combination of confusion and desire in his eyes. "Hmm…if you're under my spell, then you must follow my orders."

Mark ducked his head and nipped her top lip. "Enchanted, yes. Enslaved, no."

Faith let out an exaggerated sigh. "You're no fun."

He chuckled and gave her a light kiss. "Just wait until I've got you in my bed. Then you'll see what fun is."

He froze, blinked, then shook his head and groaned. "Now you have me spouting lines like some B-movie character."

Faith laughed. That stuffy Mark Tonelli felt comfortable enough to play with her sent warmth of an entirely different sort spiraling through her veins. And here she'd thought this was going to be an intense, hot affair. Not something so playful that it touched a long-starved part of herself and made her feel fully alive for the first time in years.

Even before Lyndi's death, Faith realized she'd shut part of herself off from the world. The better to get the story without suffering an emotional breakdown every time the people involved experienced joy, sorrow or pain. Outside of the job, Faith had hung out with friends and taken lovers, leading her to believe she'd been handling her life perfectly well.

But Mark made her see that she'd remained emotionally frozen even after giving up her job.

"I'm melting, I'm melting," she murmured.

"I should hope so," he replied.

Faith just shook her head, not surprised that he'd missed the movie reference. "Modest, aren't you?"

"No. I don't see the point."

Yeah, that fit. The man knew his worth, and if he seemed to think himself better than most, well, she didn't really know him well enough to say differently. Pulling herself out of serious self-analysis mode, she nuzzled against Mark and licked a damp trail from his collarbone down to his nipple.

He sucked in a breath and took two lunging steps forward. Then the world spun and her back landed on the softness of a mattress. While she'd been deep in thought, Mark had reached the top floor and carried her into his bedroom. She barely had time to register soft light shining on dark wood furniture before Mark, naked—somehow he'd managed to shuck his pants without her noticing—crawled onto the bed and hooked the fingers of one hand under the waistband of her skirt.

With a strong tug, he pulled off her pantyhose and panties, then slid her skirt down her legs, leaving her bare to his gaze.

"I can't believe you're here. In my bed," Mark breathed. "So beautiful. So right."

Gone was the playful, teasing man of a moment ago. His eyes stared into hers with a heated intensity that stole all her thoughts and incinerated the oxygen in her lungs. Something deep inside snapped, as if Mark had broken through an unknown barrier. Yet at the same time, she felt as if she were falling into his soul.

No matter how arrogant or unkind he could be, there was more good in Mark than he realized. Otherwise, he wouldn't allow her this deep stare that laid bare their vulnerabilities and opened them both up to exploitation. He wouldn't have such a look of awe on his face. And the kiss he gave her wouldn't promise safety and security and yes, even love.

Just when she thought she couldn't bear the overwhelming sense of being stripped bare to her soul, Mark kissed her harder. Wildness took over and the tenderness they'd just shared burned away under the sheer heat of desire.

She'd thought him urbane and controlled, but the hint of danger she'd sensed in him now came roaring out. He kissed her like he wanted to devour her. To absorb every bit of her essence through his mouth. Faith clutched his back and strained to get closer as her body ignited. She couldn't breathe. The kiss stole all her oxygen, but she didn't want to relinquish Mark's mouth to take a deep breath.

Her heart felt like it had been possessed. But she needed this. Needed to be closer to Mark. To feel this sense that she finally could let go and just feel. That despite barely knowing him, Mark wouldn't let her down. She could let herself enjoy the moment without wallowing in guilt or grief and Mark wouldn't judge her for it. When he lifted his head, she made a sound of protest and tried to pull his mouth back down to hers.

But he had other plans. His mouth skimmed down her throat to her chest, his lips sucking and his teeth nipping as he went. Until his mouth settled on her breast. The powerful suction, combined with his clever fingers shaping and plucking at her other breast, had her arching off the bed. A moment later his fingers delved between her thighs, finding and spreading the moisture there, then teasing her clit.

"Mark!" She was so close to coming already. "I want you inside me."

But instead of his cock, she felt two fingers slide inside her, testing her readiness. She writhed against him, needing more pressure. Mark ignored her silent request, keeping his mouth on her breast while he slowly worked his fingers in and out of her until she was riding the edge of an orgasm. She grabbed his ears and raised his face so she could glare at him

"Fuck me already, damn you!"

His pupils expanded and he inhaled sharply. She had a moment to wonder why her swearing turned him on as he grabbed for a condom and sheathed himself. Then he moved over her body and slid inside.

"Yes!" Faith closed her eyes, reveling in the sense of fullness that was almost, but not quite, too much to bear. She pressed her head harder into the pillow as she shifted to get a better angle to take him deep.

"Are you all right?" he murmured.

She wet her lips and nodded, but didn't open her eyes. She wanted this to be all about physical sensation. She didn't think she could handle any more deeply tender emotional moments.

She dug her fingers into his firm buttocks and urged him forward. With a guttural moan, he took her mouth in another bruising kiss, then began to slowly move in and out of her.

"Mmm...faster."

His tempo barely speeded up. "Like this?"

Her eyes flew open. "Are you kidding me? You're going to tease me now?" She hissed in frustration and scored him lightly with her nails. "Either speed up and make me come, or I'll finish the job myself."

To prove her point, she slipped her hand in between their bodies and squeezed her clit.

"Oh no, you don't," Mark growled. He jerked her hand away and pinned it over her head, then pinned her other hand up as well. "You want to be fucked, I'll fuck you. But you damn well won't need any help to come."

Faith tipped her head to one side and raised her eyebrow. "I'm hearing a lot of talk, Mr. Tonelli. Can you—" Mark slammed into her then withdrew quickly. "Oh!" He set a new, faster rhythm that had her hips rising to meet his and her head thrashing against the bed.

She struggled to pull her hands free, but Mark's grip was unbreakable.

"Want to...touch...you," she gasped. "Please!" She couldn't bear the pressure any longer. She needed release. Now. Or she was going to die.

"No. Wanted a...slow...seduction." Each word was punctuated by a thrust of his hips. "Wanted...to prove...not...just lust. Now...you've got...to pay...the consequences." He lowered his mouth to her throat and nipped.

The stinging pain sent her over the edge. Her body bowed

off the bed and she screamed. Mark pressed harder on her wrists and captured her mouth in another fierce kiss and the sense of being restrained only ratcheted the pleasure higher.

Then Mark went rigid and cried out and another orgasm hit her.

The world pulsed behind her eyelids in a display of brilliant colors, until the pleasure ebbed on an outgoing wave, leaving her limp and satiated.

"Oh...my...God..." she murmured, stroking her hand down Mark's back as he sprawled on top of her. "That was..."

"Amazing," he breathed.

She managed a weak laugh, surprised she had the energy for even that. "Yeah." She pressed a kiss to the damp skin of his neck.

He grunted, then rolled off her. Faith opened her mouth to protest the loss of his heat, but he snaked his arm around her waist and pulled her snug against his side. They lay in peaceful silence, something she hadn't expected to find, particularly not with a man so closely tied to Jamieson.

Thankful she wasn't alone, and marveling that in the midst of her frantic hunt for Toby she'd found someone to trust, she listened to Mark's heartbeat slow until sleep dragged her under.

CHAPTER SEVEN

FAITH WOKE SLOWLY, wrapped in Mark's arms, the comforter tucked under her chin. After their first bout of lovemaking she'd slept, only to be awakened by Mark's kisses. He'd proceeded to do things to her with his lips and tongue that even now sent heat spiraling into her belly. She didn't think she'd ever clicked sexually with a man the way she did with Mark. She smiled drowsily.

"You're thinking too much," he murmured against her ear.

Faith laughed. "Once upon a time I would have said I'm thinking too little. Here I am, in bed with a man I barely know. One who works with the man I believe may have kidnapped my brother. On the surface, that doesn't seem very smart." Yet her little voice of reason was quiet, lulled into contentment after hours of lovemaking. Her head felt clearer. Her heart...well, it wasn't lighter, not with Toby in trouble, but she didn't feel on the verge of hopelessness.

Or maybe it was just that her instincts continued to insist that Mark was a true ally.

"Hmm." Mark nuzzled her neck. "One might say that becoming involved with a reporter—"

"Former reporter."

"No. From the few journalists I've known, one is born a newshound and stays a newshound until death." He nipped her chin. "As I was saying, my getting involved with a reporter is not exactly a wise move. How do I know you're not going to spill all my secrets in an exposé?"

Faith leaned back so she could look him in the eye. "Do you really think that?"

He shook his head and gave her a soft kiss on her forehead. "No. For some indescribable reason, my instincts tell me that my secrets are safe with you."

She smiled and kissed him. Which led to roving hands and deeper, more urgent kisses. A long while later, after the sweat had cooled from their skin and Faith was once again nestled against Mark, he cleared his throat.

"I've read the news reports, but I want to hear your version of what happened with your sister. Why did you give up your career?"

Panic shot through her. Faith jerked away from him and sat up.

"Faith." Mark's soothing voice calmed her. The warmth and understanding in his eyes relaxed her even further. He wasn't asking about her story so he could judge her, but because he cared and wanted to know her better.

She had to admit that if they were going to move forward into a relationship then he deserved to know. She lay back down and let Mark gather her close to his body. Somehow it was easier to talk without having to watch his expression. Yet she found she couldn't find the words to start.

"Go back to the beginning and tell your story as if I don't know the basics," Mark finally prompted. "I want your interpretation, not the impersonal words from a report."

Okay. She could do this.

"I used to be an investigative journalist," she began. "I traveled all over the world covering humanitarian issues and political events. I spent probably ninety percent of my time away from my tiny apartment in Washington, D.C."

Mark stroked his hand down her back. "You're originally from Ohio?"

"Yes. Dalioma, Ohio. Dad was a cop. Mom taught music at the high school and led the marching band. I'm the middle child. Toby is the oldest and Lyndi was the baby, ten years younger than me."

Even just saying her sister's name made her throat tighten. How was she supposed to get through the entire story? But Mark didn't pressure her to continue, so she swallowed the pain and forced herself to go on.

"Lyndi started sending me letters while I was in college and continued writing after my newspaper assignments kept me overseas. Once she hit middle school her letters changed. She stopped writing pages about her friends and what happened at school, and instead wrote long, rambling paragraphs describing how much she missed me, how unhappy she was, and begging me to visit her."

Faith sighed. "Most of the time her letters arrived weeks after she'd mailed them, finding me in whatever city I'd made my temporary base. The few times I went home, Lyndi was so happy to see me I felt guilty for having being away so long." She still dreamed of Lyndi's face, radiant with joy when she'd met her plane that last time.

"But..." Guilt clogged her throat. She coughed, then continued. "The hard truth was that after a few days, Lyndi's constant attention started to smother me and I'd be itching to leave."

"Sounds natural," Mark commented.

"I thought so." Now, she wondered whether she'd sensed the storm brewing in her sister and had just been too much of a coward to deal with it.

"Anyway, time passed and Lyndi entered high school. Her

letters became very infrequent, but when she did write she talked of not fitting in at home or at school. How she was never good enough for my parents. In more than one letter she accused me of not loving her, because if I loved her I'd stop traveling and stay home with her."

Even now, Faith questioned her decision to put career before family. If she'd stayed home, could she have stopped what happened? The psychologists told her it wasn't her fault. That Lyndi had been responsible for her own actions. But Faith was the big sister. It was her job to protect her little sister and she'd failed miserably.

"The letters from my parents mentioned that they were having trouble with Lyndi. A few of her relationships were abusive. One boyfriend even put her in the hospital with a broken rib. She'd gotten into fights several times at school and once got picked up for drunk driving, but their letters made it sound like nothing more than immaturity. A way for Lyndi to assert her independence after being the baby of the family for so long."

In hindsight, Faith understood that Lyndi's acting out had been an attempt to convince herself that her parents loved her, no matter what she did.

"Then Toby unexpectedly showed up at a refugee camp in Jordan where I was interviewing women who'd fled the Syrian civil war." The heat had been relentless that day. She could still remember the sun-baked tightness of the skin on her face and the prickle of sweat meandering down her spine.

"Toby dragged me to an isolated section of the camp and told me that Lyndi had gotten hold of a gun, waited for our parents to come home, then shot them before turning the gun on herself. All three were dead when the police arrived."

The sun had glared down out of a brilliant blue sky as if judging Faith for not saving her sister. As Toby's words had sunk in, goose bumps had sprouted on her arms despite the temperature.

"I'm so sorry." Mark's arm tightened around her and she realized that this was the first time she'd told the story to someone who was a complete outsider. His concern soothed some of the pain of telling the story.

"You blamed yourself," he said. "For not being home."

"Yeah." She liked the way Mark didn't try and pass judgment on her self-condemnation.

"And that's why you hate guns."

"Right again. I used to carry a gun on assignments, depending on what part of the world I was in. More often than not I had at least one knife on my body in addition to a gun. But after Lyndi's death, I haven't wanted to be near a gun."

"Until you decided to hold one on me."

Faith could hear the amusement in his tone. "Yes. I was desperate, so I picked up one of Toby's emergency weapons." Her lips kicked up in a smile. "That's something you have in common. You've both planned ahead, assuming there will come a day when you need to go on the run."

She laughed at the frozen look on Mark's face. "Maybe that's why we get along so well," she teased. "You remind me of my brother."

"I am *not* your brother." Mark's arm shot out and snagged her around the waist, pulling her flush against him. His mouth plundered hers in a thoroughly carnal kiss, and his intensely possessive grip left no doubt that he considered her to be his woman. A walled off section of Faith's heart cracked open. Despite the danger, despite coming from two different worlds —he lived in the shadows and she exposed those shadows to the light—she'd never felt so cherished or protected.

When Mark finally let her go, Faith couldn't stop the broad grin of feminine satisfaction that stretched her cheeks. Giving him a peck on the lips, she snuggled against him.

"What I don't understand," Mark said, running his hand down her hair, "is why you gave up journalism. I've read some of your pieces. You're a talented writer. Skilled at bringing the subject alive in a way that makes an emotional connection with the reader. Your compassion leaps off the page."

Damn, how did he always know the right thing to say? Did they teach him that during CIA agent training?

"The local press tore our family apart," Faith replied once she'd swallowed down the lump of emotion in her throat. "Every aspect of our lives was sifted through and made public, no matter how irrelevant. Someone even broke in and stole Lyndi's diaries, then published entries in such a way as to make them seem like indictments based on fact, rather than the emotional outpourings of a distressed teen. The majority of articles painted all of us as guilty of the crime. Even my parents came under attack. The press decided that our treatment of Lyndi had fed her depression, even though there had never been any emotional or physical abuse. In fact, as the baby of the family, Lyndi was given more leniency than either Toby or me. We all loved her and tended to spoil her. So I don't understand why she started to believe that no one loved her. When the police finally tracked down the diaries and returned them to us, I read the entire four books."

Faith's eyes grew damp. "In the diaries you could see the progression. See how Lyndi's insecurities grew like a cancer, twisting even the most innocent exchange into an attack against her by an uncaring world. But that's not how the media portrayed her. They portrayed her as a victim whose pleas for help had been ignored."

Her old anger bubbled up. "That was bullshit. My parents did everything they could to help Lyndi. They talked to her. Got other adults Lyndi respected to speak to her. They even took her to counseling. But Lyndi..." Faith's voice cracked. "She didn't want to be helped. She enjoyed playing the martyr too much. Of course, the media ran with the martyr idea, ignoring the complexity of the situation. Because the truth didn't fit neatly into the allotted sound bite."

She shivered. "I wasn't naïve. While I always tried to treat the people involved in my stories with the dignity and respect they deserved, particularly if I was interacting with them during a period of grief, I knew not all of my colleagues acted with compassion. I fully understood that false or unfair reporting by some unscrupulous journalists created additional victims. Still, it was a shock when my family and I became the target of hostile and sensational reporting."

"I'm sorry." Mark placed a kiss on her hair and Faith let the warmth of his concern wash through her, blunting the lingering pain of the memory.

"Toby had taken leave from the army in order to attend the funerals, but all too soon he had to return to duty. Leaving me and my grandma to deal with the harassment. Maybe because I was a colleague, the reporters were hardest on me. They made my life hell for three months. It left a sour taste in my mouth regarding the entire profession. Made me question whether there was any honor left in journalism. For the first time in my life I was ashamed to admit that I was a reporter."

The shame had mixed with guilt over not being there for Lyndi, causing Faith to veer dangerously close to clinical depression. Only the support of her grandma and friends like Siobahn, combined with productive sessions with an experienced psychologist had kept her functioning and eventually helped her regain her perspective.

"The whole ordeal also made me question why it was easier for me to investigate events overseas than to deal with family issues," Faith admitted. "So I decided to give up my career and do what Lyndi had always wanted me to do. I settled down and put family first."

Sometimes she wondered if Lyndi would be angry that it took her death to make Faith finally stay home.

"At first I stayed in my hometown, but after Gramma died there were too many memories. Too many people who wanted to talk about Lyndi and no one that I cared deeply about to hold me there. So I moved to a small town in Maryland not far from D.C. I teach journalism at the local college and run the high school newspaper. I try to make sure my students understand that the press has a responsibility to behave with sensitivity toward individuals. That the truth shouldn't come at the expense of trampling people's dignity and privacy into the ground."

Mark gave a small snort. "That's the difference between our professions. People are just pawns in the intelligence game. Yes, we claim that our ultimate goal is to make the world safe for the ordinary citizen, but that's not really why successful agents continue to do this work. We like manipulating. Like working within the protection of the shadows and not having to follow the rules that constrain the rest of society."

"That sounds cold. And lonely."

"No. It's a power rush when you outmaneuver an enemy and gain the information he'd worked so hard to hide. A rush that I suspect is as addictive as cocaine. I've lived most of my life working to get the next rush. The more dangerous the mission, the stronger the rush."

She couldn't stop herself from asking, "But don't you ever get lonely?"

Mark put his fingers against her cheek and turned her face so that he could look into her eyes. "No. I've never been a particularly social man. Most people hold little interest for me beyond what they have to offer in respect to my job. I've never had problems finding female companions and have never wanted more than a shallow, physical relationship with them."

Faith's stupid heart sank.

"Until you."

Joy. A brilliant smile threatened to split Faith's face. She kissed him and that led to more loving, which this time felt deeper. Richer. She might have fallen too hard, too fast, but damn if she wasn't going to hold on to Mark for as long as she could.

CHAPTER EIGHT

Nine Days Later

"Abernathy," Mark called to the guard who'd recently been assigned to Kerberos.

"Sir?"

At first glance, the man appeared the same as any other guard. Military short haircut. Clean shaven. Erect posture. But his eyes when they met yours were a little too wary. Too much like a puppy waiting to be kicked. And he moved gingerly, as if he couldn't quite control the faster movements of his body.

The man supposedly had been put through a new program by Dr. Kaufmann. This one wasn't meant to bulk men up and turn them into powerful, nearly indestructible soldiers. Instead, the new program aimed to create a faster, more intelligent spy and assassin. Mark knew that Dr. Nevsky had originally been tasked by the CIA to produce super spies and assassins, just as the DOD had wanted Nevsky to give them super soldiers. Apparently Kaufmann had decided to add the spies to his program against Jamieson's wishes, although Mark's boss had agreed to give the newly enhanced men a try.

Thus Abernathy's assignment to the administrative side of Kerberos. "Touchdown Tiger Rose," Mark said.

Abernathy straightened and a blank look came over his face. "Ready for orders, sir."

"You have a key to Jamieson's office?"

"Yes, sir."

"Good." Mark swallowed the bitterness at the back of his mouth. "I want you to go into Jamieson's office and bring me a copy of the contents of the folder labeled *Test Subjects* that is in the bottom right desk drawer." While he suspected that during their last meeting Jamieson had placed the folder in the drawer as a test to see if Mark would try to access the contents, he couldn't pass up this opportunity. It was the first hard proof he'd seen that tied Jamieson to Kaufmann.

He handed Abernathy a camera. "Take pictures of the documents inside the folder with this. I am particularly interested in a list of names I believe you will find there. Also, I want copies of any other files relating to Kerberos and Kaufmann's lab. You will not speak about my request or otherwise give any indication to another person regarding what I have asked you to do. Understood?"

Abernathy's eyes held the unfocused look of a dreamer, making Mark's stomach churn as the man saluted. "Yes, sir!"

"Very good. Jamieson is out of the building right now, along with his personal guards. Work as fast as you can, then return to me when you have completed your task."

"Yes, sir."

Mark watched the man speed walk down the hall, before returning to his desk. Jamieson had requested that he put together a list of potential clients who might be interested in purchasing the enhanced men to supplement their roster of personal bodyguards or to bulk up their private armies. Mark used his knowledge of the underworld of Russia and Eastern

Europe to make a start on the list, but he couldn't fully focus due to uncharacteristic nerves.

His unease wasn't because this was his best chance to find out if Jamieson had authorized Toby's abduction. Rather, he didn't want to let Faith down. And at this point, his key priorities included passing on any information that would help the SSU locate and destroy Kaufmann's lab.

When a knock came on his door ten minutes later, Mark flinched even though he'd been expecting it. "You're back faster than I estimated," he said as he ushered Abernathy inside, then closed the door behind him.

Abernathy handed over a new file folder containing still warm photocopies of the requested documents. He placed the camera on Mark's desk. "I used the personal copy machine inside the office," he said by way of explanation.

"Thank you." Mark hadn't realized that the enhanced spies and assassins retained their capacity for independent thought, but on further reflection, that made sense. Spying and assassination required subtlety and an ability to think quickly on your feet. Which meant this new category of enhanced men posed a greater threat than the overly muscular, violent soldiers Kaufmann turned out. A side effect of the military side of the program resulted in the altered soldiers thinking at a child's level, unable to independently process and follow through on complex ideas without receiving commands directly from their handlers.

"Abernathy!" The bellow of the chief of security filtered through even the thick door of Mark's office.

Abernathy turned ice white. "Hide me. Please!" He clutched at Mark's arm. "You don't know what he'll do to me if he finds out that I obeyed an order from someone else."

"You had no choice."

The guard shook his head. "It doesn't matter. He can't find

out! Please. Help me." His eyes pleaded with Mark, his terror evident.

Mark hesitated. His mission was greater than one man. In the cutthroat intelligence game, sometimes individuals needed to be sacrificed in order to achieve results that would benefit all of society.

But he was no longer a man who could turn a blind eye to Abernathy's fear. What if this had been Toby? How would he explain to Faith that he hadn't done everything in his power to help protect the man?

Mark took a deep breath, realizing that this decision might destroy all his hard work toward getting revenge on Jamieson. "There's a back door out of my office into a secure stairwell," he said, indicating for Abernathy to follow him.

"Thank you!" The overwhelming gratitude and relief on the man's face made Mark uncomfortable.

Abernathy reached for the door handle.

Mark slapped his hand on top of Abernathy's. "Touchdown Tiger Rose," he snapped.

Abernathy went still.

"You will forget you met with me," Mark ordered. "You will forget everything that happened since I called your name. You will take the hidden staircase to the exterior, at which point you will leave this facility and its grounds and never speak of our encounter again."

"Yes, sir." Abernathy's wooden tone caused Mark's nascent conscience to wince, but he ignored it.

"Good luck." Mark lifted his hand and let Abernathy open the door. Once the man had disappeared into the dimly lit stairwell, Mark shut and locked the door, then forced himself to return to his desk and resume work as normal.

He snuck a quick peek at the names in the report Abernathy had retrieved. Toby Andrews was listed under the heading of most recent acquisitions to Kaufmann's program.

Mark stared at the name for a moment and his heart knocked against his chest. Then he closed the file and tucked it and the other copies Abernathy had made safely away in his desk drawer.

When the second knock he'd been expecting sounded on his door, Mark schooled his features into his usual arrogant disdain. "Yes?"

"We're looking for a missing guard," the head of security announced as he stepped into the office, his gaze darting around the cramped space.

"As you can see," Mark replied coldly, letting annoyance seep into his tone, "there is no one here but me." He held his breath, but the man finished his survey without lingering on the spot where Abernathy had exited.

"Thank you, sir. Please let us know if you see this man." The security chief handed Mark a photograph. "He may have become unstable."

Mark lifted one of his brows and gave a curt nod. After one more visual check of the office, the man left.

Mark slowly blew out his breath. So, the security chief didn't know about the hidden door. Interesting. His temporary office was one of three offices hastily partitioned out of a secure conference room. Apparently, no one had realized that the original room had an escape route, or that his office had ended up with the door. Good to know.

Hoping that Abernathy had made it outside without being spotted, Mark continued working until his normal quitting time several hours later. When he finally shut down his computer and headed toward the elevators, he ended up behind a group of administrative staff.

"Did you hear?" one of them whispered loudly to her friend. "Abernathy failed his assignment. They decided he wasn't stable enough to handle being a guard here. They sent him back to his training facility."

A chill raced through Mark.

"Such a shame. He was a hottie."

The first woman giggled. "Yeah. Weird, but definitely fantasy material."

The women turned down a corridor, leaving Mark with a couple of the security staff. "Heartless bitches," a man Mark had seen a few times muttered. "The guy's dead."

"Excuse me," Mark said. "Did you say that Abernathy is dead? How? When? The chief of security said he'd gone missing."

The man hesitated, as if uncertain what he was allowed to reveal.

"It's okay, George," a second man said. "He's Mark Tonelli, remember? The one who's been working directly with Jamieson."

"Ah. Right." He raised a brow. "You mean you haven't heard?"

Mark wondered if Jamieson had become aware of his use of Abernathy and decided to withhold information on the man's death. No. His boss would flaunt it. "I didn't see any alert go out," he replied.

"Wasn't an alert. We just heard about it because one of our buddies was there." The man glanced around to make certain they weren't in danger of being overheard. "They caught Abernathy trying to escape into the woods. Since his behavior was suspicious and against protocol, they decided to send him back to the training compound where he came from. My friend said he was terrified. He fought the men assigned to escort him to the transportation. Just went totally berserk and attacked his guards. In the ensuing struggle, he was shot and killed." The man shook his head. "My friend thinks Abernathy was so scared of his punishment that he chose suicide by guard instead."

An unfamiliar, icy horror seeped through Mark's veins. *My*

fault. If I hadn't ordered him to get the file for me, Abernathy would still be alive. Unused to feeling regret at the loss of life, he tamped down his uncharacteristic feelings. "That's a pity," Mark said, wishing he could say so much more. "I didn't know him, but he seemed to be a decent fellow. I'm sorry for your loss." The words tasted like ashes as they passed his lips.

The man nodded. "Thanks. He might have been one of the freaks, but he was a good guy. Didn't always get our jokes, but he really tried to fit in."

For some reason, that comment made Mark's throat tighten. Needing to be alone in order to process these strange reactions, he bid his companions good-bye and took the stairs to the parking garage.

Faith. He needed to see Faith. To hold her and have her warmth thaw this insidious cold taking over his body. Not that he deserved her compassion. Right now he hated himself.

What have I become?

FAITH KNEW something was terribly wrong when Mark let himself into the safe house. There was a bleak, dazed look of shock in his eyes that made her want to pull him into her arms and offer him the comfort of a hug. Yet the tight set of his mouth and the way his normally perfect hair showed furrows where his fingers had run through it, warned her that he was holding on to his control by a hairsbreadth. Instead, she accepted his brief kiss, then pushed him gently toward the couch while she headed for the kitchen.

She pulled down a bottle of vodka and poured a hefty dose into a tumbler, then set both glass and bottle next to him on the end table. He'd already torn off his necktie and loosened the first few buttons on his dress shirt. Grabbing the glass with the desperation of a drowning man latching onto a life preserver, he tossed the drink back with such force she wondered that he didn't give himself whiplash.

Not knowing what else to do, she curled beside Mark on the couch, letting him know silently that he wasn't alone. Only after his second drink did she venture to speak. "Can you talk about it?"

Mark sighed deeply, sank back against the cushions and put his arm around her. She glanced up and saw his head was tipped back against the sofa and his eyes were closed. "I have the list of men who were sent to Kaufmann's program," he said.

Excitement slid through her and she started to rise, but he tightened his arm. "What's wrong? Wasn't Toby's name on it?"

Mark gave a bitter laugh. "Oh, Toby was on it, all right."

Faith's heart lifted, then immediately sank. If Toby was still alive, why was Mark so upset? "What has you so wrung out?"

"It's..." Mark sighed. He opened his eyes and looked down at her. There was something lost in his gaze that made her heart clench. "It's what I had to do to get the list."

He shifted his glance to the ceiling. "I am not a good person, Faith. People call me arrogant. Cold. Ruthless. All of which is true. I purposely became those things in order to pursue revenge for my father's murder."

Mark fell silent and Faith waited patiently for him to continue.

He took a healthy sip of vodka. "I've never cared much for other people's feelings or their opinion of me unless they were important to my goals. Hurting or killing people who stood in my way has never bothered me. In fact, if you'd asked me three months ago if I possessed a conscience, I would have said no. But what I saw in Moscow at Dr. Ivanov's lab changed me."

Mark reached out and poured himself another shot of vodka. "When I saw what Ivanov had forced his patients to become, I felt empathy. Pity. Anger on behalf of his subjects. I knew I had to stand against such abuse of the human mind and body. What I did today..."

He shook his head and she felt the motion in her soul. "Did you kill someone you liked?"

"No. Worse. There was a guard at our office who had graduated from a new part of Kaufmann's program. A program with the goal of creating super spies and assassins. The man was undergoing a trial period to see whether he could blend in with normal colleagues." He took another shot of vodka.

"I overheard one of the supervisors giving the man an order that was prefaced by an odd phrase. It didn't take much to realize that using that phrase activated the man's mind control. Whoever spoke to the man using the correct code would be able to order the man to do anything at all. So—" His chest heaved. "I used that phrase to order the man to bring me the data I needed."

"But—"

"I took away the man's will," he snapped. "I gave him an order I knew would probably bring him to the attention of the other guards. I deliberately ordered him to access Jamieson's office and bring out a copy of the list of who was in Kaufmann's program, plus any information on Kerberos and Kaufmann's lab he could find." He made a sound of disgust. "I sent him into danger that I wasn't willing to risk."

"But you didn't have access to the office, did you?"

"That's not the point!" Mark's vodka glass sailed across the room and shattered against the fireplace. "I hate what's been done to these men. Faith, at Ivanov's lab I witnessed a man bludgeoning his brother to death. The look of confusion, then horror in his eyes as he stared at his victim still haunts me. You've never seen such torment in a man's eyes. Tears streamed down his face and he sobbed with each blow he delivered. He even begged the scientists to let him stop. But they ignored him.

The head scientist bragged to me that they'd finally found the key to break down the man's resistance. I never thought..."

A muscle in his jaw twitched and his lips firmed as he cut off whatever he'd been about to say. "I realized then that there are some lines even I consider inviolable. Interfering with men's minds and bodies to this extent is one of those lines." He grimaced. "Kaufmann's program might even be worse than Ivanov's."

Part of her didn't want to hear any more. Didn't want further proof that Toby might be so fundamentally changed that he'd never return to being the big brother she knew and loved. But she owed it to him not to shy away from the truth, no matter if it turned her stomach.

"Think about it, Faith. If Kaufmann has created a trigger, anyone with knowledge of the key phrase can give orders to the enhanced men, just like I did. Abernathy didn't have a choice but to obey me. What if I'd asked him to kill an innocent?"

Faith shivered.

"See?" Mark said. "You hate the idea of mind control, too. How could any decent human being not be afraid of being turned into nothing more than a slave based on certain words being spoken?" He picked up the vodka bottle and took a long drag.

"Yet at the first opportunity, I became just like the scientists, manipulating one of their subjects to get me the information I needed. So much for my reawakened conscience. At heart, I'm as selfish and cowardly as ever."

Faith lightly caressed his chest with her fingers. She'd never seen him this emotional before. "Shh, I'm sure it's not as bad as you think. He—"

"He handed over the papers and turned to go. Just then we heard his supervisor hollering for him. God. I'll never forget the terror in his eyes. He looked at me, begging me to save him from the man's wrath. I knew then that I'd made a mistake. That helping me could cost him his life."

His self-recrimination surprised Faith. Mark wasn't one to doubt himself.

"I showed him the secret exit out of my office, then ordered Abernathy to forget everything I'd said to him. They caught him, Faith." He grabbed her hand and squeezed so hard she gave a squeak of pain. "Killed him." His chest heaved. "The story is that he went berserk as they were taking him out to the transport that would return him to Kaufmann. That he died in the ensuing fight. I think he was so terrified of being returned to Kaufmann that he attacked his escorts and provoked them into killing him. Either that, or they outright executed him and the berserker story was just a cover."

"Oh, God, Mark, that's horrible. I'm so sorry."

"Sorry won't bring the man back. I should have done more to help him. Created a diversion. Or found a place to hide him, then asked the SSU to come pick him up. Their doctors have experience counteracting Kaufmann's drugs. But no, I couldn't risk it. Couldn't. Risk . It. Letting him use the escape route was as far as I was willing to go. When did I become such a fucking coward?!"

Faith flinched at Mark's uncharacteristically crude language. "What else could you have done?" she murmured after she'd let several minutes pass in silence. "You had no way of knowing they'd catch him, let alone kill him."

"The danger was so great, I couldn't risk going into Jamieson's office myself, but I had no compunction about ordering Abernathy to do it. Don't you see? I judged his life to be worth less than mine," Mark shot back. "What kind of man does that make me?" His laugh was bitter. "Not a man who deserves you."

"Mark, I—"

"What? Because of me a man is dead. Don't you understand? Because I gave Abernathy no choice on how to act, he wasn't able to save himself."

Tears filled Faith's eyes. The dead man could so easily have been Toby. She grabbed a tissue, then turned her face away from Mark while she blew her nose and dabbed at her eyes. Crying wouldn't help her brother. And if they could find Kaufmann's lab, not only could they rescue Toby, but they could free all the other victims as well.

"You hate me, don't you?" Mark asked quietly.

Faith spun around and glared at him. "Whatever makes you say that?"

"I—" The confusion and fragile hope in his eyes reminded Faith that his life had been deficient of unconditional love.

"Mark, you did the best you could with the information you had. You tried to help Abernathy escape. Stop blaming yourself." Faith couldn't stand hearing the pain in his voice. Pain she bet most people never saw, because he hid it so well under a thick veneer of arrogance. She reached out and stroked his cheek. "Two months ago would you have even tried to help the man?"

Mark shook his head.

"See? No matter what you've done in the past, you're now a better man than you think." She leaned forward and pressed her lips gently to his. "And I still like for you. Very much."

"Oh, God. Thank you." Mark pulled her into a crushing hug.

A long while later, he released her. Looked down at her with a renewed strength and peace. "You're too good for me, Faith."

She gave him a saucy smile. "Maybe. But you're not getting rid of me that easily." Then she sobered. "We still need to rescue Toby and the others from Kaufmann. So, where is he being held?"

Mark pushed to his feet and paced across the room, stopping in front of the bookcase next to the fireplace. He picked up one of the seashells she'd placed on the top shelf in an attempt to make the safe house a little bit more homey.

"That's the problem, Faith," he said after he'd arranged the shells in a precise line, biggest to smallest. "All I managed to obtain was a list of men who have already been sent to Kaufmann. I still don't know the location of the lab. Now do you get it? Abernathy died in vain, because we're no closer now to finding Toby and Kaufmann's lab than we were yesterday!"

Faith stood up and walked over to him, then wrapped her arms around his waist and pressed her body against his back.

He turned and pulled her into his arms.

"But at least we know he's alive," she said. "Or was alive until recently. That's something."

"Not anything good. Faith, stop fooling yourself. We're not talking about mild, easily-reversible changes to your brother's mind and body. If we find Toby, he won't be the same man you remember. He's more likely to be a monster."

How dare he feel sorry for her? But then, he'd already admitted to being stunted when it came to caring for another person. He couldn't possibly understand what it meant to love someone so much you'd do anything to protect them. "Mark, no matter what shape he's in, Toby is my brother. I'm going to bring him home." She took a deep breath. "But if the guard was killed just because he helped you, then you're in danger. I—"

Mark placed his finger over her lips. "Don't even try to suggest that I give up now, Faith. I'm still going to help you. I just wanted to make sure you understand that if we do rescue Toby from the program, he might try to kill you."

She bit her lip, then nodded.

"There is some hope. The SSU has been collaborating with a scientist who defected from Kaufmann's program. She's been working toward reversing the damage done to one of their soldiers. Maybe she'll be able to help Toby."

"Thank you. I...I'll never be able to repay you for all of your help. He's...he's not just the only family I have left, but he's my best friend. He's the only one in the family who supported my career. And he never blamed me for not giving in to Lyndi's demands to return home. I don't know how I'll keep going if I lose him."

Mark's hands tightened on her back. "I don't want thanks, Faith. Don't you understand? I care about you. All I want is to make you happy."

She thought she'd used up all of her tears during her breakdown the other evening on the beach. But at Mark's kindness, Faith started crying.

"Don't cry, sweetheart. Please don't cry. It hurts." Mark sounded so baffled by his empathy that Faith gave a watery laugh. Then she pushed away from his chest and looked up at him. When she'd started her search for Toby she'd had no idea that she'd end up meeting a man who could look at her with such tenderness. A man that she knew, despite his flaws, would die to protect her.

"I know it's too soon, but I've never felt this way before. I love you, Mark." She laughed at the stunned look in his eyes. "Um. Sorry. I—"

Mark's lips took hers in a bruising kiss. "Say it again."

"I love you Mark."

He kissed her again. "I don't know anything about love. I don't know if I'm actually capable of love. But what I feel for you?" He shook his head. "It's beyond my control. I can't imagine life without you. If that's love, then I love you."

Her heart soared. "Oh, God, I didn't expect this. Not now. Not with you. But I'm so glad not to be alone in how I feel."

"Me, too." With shocking quickness, Mark scooped her up into his arms and carried her upstairs. Then he proved that despite his lack of experience, he understood love very well.

CHAPTER NINE

One Week Later

MARK STARED out the window of his car. Once again he'd retreated to the safety of a lone stretch of public park. Only this time, he was trying to get his game face on before he returned to the safe house and Faith.

He shook his head and ran his fingers through his hair. For the first time since they'd met, he had to withhold critical information from Faith. The prospect of lying to her about what he'd just learned ate him up inside. A bitter laugh escaped. Telling lies or omitting key information were critical components of his job. He'd never minded before. But now that he'd met Faith and become used to sharing his thoughts and his past with her, he hated knowing that he couldn't tell her about the President's involvement in the upcoming attack.

He sighed and got out of the car, needing to move in order to settle his nerves. Since when did he suffer from nerves? His reputation of being a cold-hearted bastard was taking a serious hit. All because he'd fallen in love.

Not that he'd give up Faith for anything. But their relationship was definitely a complication. Mainly because she was a reporter and the news he'd received today was potentially explosive.

According to Jamieson, the President had requested that teams of enhanced Kerberos soldiers participate in an upcoming assault against an island in the Pacific. Mark at first had refused to believe it. No matter how badly the President wanted to get revenge against the terrorists who'd killed his son five years ago, retaliating against the entire island where the terrorists lived was the act of a man out of touch with his humanity. It would result in the deaths of thousands of innocent people.

Would Toby be part of the attack? Probably, but Mark didn't know for sure.

He strode along the boardwalk, but found no solace in the crash of the waves against the shore. He knew Faith's reporter instincts would sense his lie if he outright told her there was no update regarding her brother or Kerberos. Hopefully, she'd be satisfied to learn that Toby's notes had been correct when they suggested that the President planned an upcoming show of force.

After that, Mark would have to play it by ear. Either he'd have to lie and tell her that he didn't know the details of the attack, which was mostly true, or he'd have to explain that he couldn't reveal any additional information because it was classified. Neither of which would earn him any good will from Faith.

He sighed and kicked a seashell out of his way. Before he'd left the office, Mark had called Ryker at the SSU and passed on the information about the attack. Unfortunately, Jamieson had not revealed the name of the targeted island. To his surprise, Ryker had already heard rumors about the anniversary demonstration. He'd asked Mark to search for the name of the island, plus any information regarding the poison the Kerberos teams were going to put into the island's water supply. The SSU's scientists would then attempt to create a counteragent.

Unfortunately, Ryker had also relayed the information that Dr. Montague, the woman who'd reversed the effects of Kaufmann's program on SSU agent Rafe Andros, had been kidnapped. The SSU assumed she'd been taken by Kerberos and returned to Dr. Kaufmann.

Which meant that finding the location of the lab was now doubly important. Without Dr. Montague's help, there was little chance that Toby would ever return to being the brother Faith knew and loved. Of course, Ryker couldn't guarantee that even if the SSU rescued Dr. Montague she'd be in any condition to work. But Mark refused to dwell on that now. First he had to locate the damn lab.

He stopped and stared out at the ocean. Should he even tell Faith about Dr. Montague?

After a long moment, he decided that he had no choice. From what he'd heard about relationships, trust and honesty were important. Faith was already going to be angry with him for withholding information about the attack. He wouldn't keep her in the dark regarding Dr. Montague, as well.

Besides, knowing the doctor had been kidnapped would keep Faith focused on uncovering the location of the lab and hopefully keep her mind off of the attack.

He just had to hope that when Faith did discover the details that he'd withheld, her generous heart would forgive him.

Because as uncomfortable as he sometimes felt with all these new emotions, he did not want to go back to being the man he'd been before he met her.

"Something big is definitely going on," Siobahn said the next time Faith called her.

"Like what?" Faith stood at the edge of a decorative pond set in the middle of a public garden and watched the ducks swim by.

"I'm investigating a couple of other stories that touch on the military and no one will talk to me, even though some of those sources were the ones who first encouraged me to dig deeper. It's like they all sense something bad is about to happen and are slamming all doors shut."

Faith thought back to Toby's notes and to the argument she'd had with Mark last night.

"What type of attack?" Faith asked. "Where? Against what target?"

"I can't tell you that!" Mark shouted. "I would if I could, but damn it, this is a matter of national security and I'm not authorized to share the information."

Faith blinked, not used to seeing Mark lose his temper. Oddly, his anger cooled her own ire. Replacing fury with an icy sense of betrayal. "You don't trust me because I'm a reporter." The pain struck deep. She'd thought the connection between her and Mark had been strong enough to bind them together no matter what.

"Don't you dare start accusing me," he shot back. "You need plausible deniability if everything goes wrong. Do you really want to give them another excuse to kill you?"

"So you're doing this to protect me? Or is it really to protect your reputation? Lord forbid that the super spy Mark Tonelli get caught in an affair with a reporter."

"No! Faith, I don't give a damn about my reputation. All I want is to keep you safe."

Mark had grabbed her and kissed her, then made love to her with fierce possessiveness. Still, Faith couldn't get past the feeling that he would have given her more information regarding the President's upcoming attack if she hadn't been a journalist.

Faith sighed. "Listen, Siobahn, I'm not supposed to tell you this, but my contact says the President has authorized an upcoming attack against some undisclosed target. Kerberos soldiers will be involved."

"Wait. That sounds familiar—"

Faith heard the rustle of papers before Siobahn continued. "Yeah, here it is. Four months ago, President MacAdam held a press conference regarding the summit talks with the Association of Southeast Asian Nations. At the end of his speech, he made an offhand reference to an upcoming show of force that would show the world that the United States is not a country to forgive or forget the wrongs perpetrated against it."

"What? When? How come I didn't hear about that?"

"The statement didn't get much airtime. MacAdam had just finished talking when an aide rushed into the room with news that a series of tornadoes had devastated the Southwest. The only reason I remembered is because I was in the press room when the President spoke. The phrasing struck me as odd, and the topic unrelated to what had been mainly economic talks with ASEAN, so I included the statement in my notes as something to research later."

"That's interesting, but it doesn't help us narrow down what's going on," Faith pointed out.

A little girl ran toward the edge of the pond. Leaning over the short retaining wall, she started throwing pieces of bread toward the ducks on the shoreline below. The ducks converged noisily on the food and Faith retreated, putting her finger in her ear.

"But it could explain why my contacts have gone silent," Siobahn said. "They're afraid of retaliation from the top."

"Yeah." When Faith had moved far enough away from the little girl and her parents not to be overheard and not to have to compete with the quacking, she continued, "My contact did say that there are people aware of the attack and working to stop it. But I have no idea whether he means the military, a govern-

ment law enforcement agency, or some sort of private organization."

"Okay. I—" Siobahn made a sound of frustration. "Sorry, I
have to go. Work's calling on my other phone. Let me know if
there's anything I can do to help."

"Just continue to lay low. With the confirmation of the
President's involvement in the upcoming attack, I think there's
more danger than ever."

"Right back atcha, kiddo. Talk soon."

Faith shut down the phone. She hoped they'd more than
talk soon. That this situation would be resolved before long, so
she could have lunch with Siobahn without worrying about
who was watching. All this hiding was wearing on her nerves.
Without Mark's steadying presence beside her, she didn't know
how she'd have handled her worry over Toby these past few
weeks. She only wished there was a greater chance of finding
him before the attack went down. Because she feared that if her
brother took part in the attack, he might not survive.

Four Days Later

"I'M CALLING to give you fair warning."

Ryker's statement sent Mark's senses into high alert.

"Rafe remembered the location of Kaufmann's compound.
His team is converging on the lab as we speak. You might want
to take precautionary measures."

Mark cursed softly and shut off his computer. "Thank you."
But he was speaking to a dial tone.

Moments later, he closed the door to his office and headed
down the corridor toward the elevator. It wasn't that late. There
should be lights on behind doors and an occasional person in
the hallway.

Instead, all offices and cubicles were dark and the corridor was deserted. Every hair on the back of his neck stood on end as his footsteps echoed against the walls.

Where was everybody? Had Jamieson sent all the staff home? Mark's office door was thick, so it was conceivable that everyone had left while he'd been absorbed in his work.

There could be no good reason for him being alone. Particularly not given the timing of the SSU's raid.

Mark waited impatiently for the elevator to arrive, feeling as if the shadows were moving in on him. With his back pressed against the wall, he scanned the empty hallway.

Perhaps he should grab Faith and ask the SSU for asylum. But no, he couldn't stomach the thought of running away now and letting someone else take Jamieson down. He needed to see Jamieson's eyes when he confronted him. Needed to personally avenge his father's murder.

He'd just have to proceed very carefully. Come into work tomorrow and act as if he didn't know anything about the raid on Kaufmann's compound.

The elevator dinged.

As the door slid open, Mark took one last probing look around the corridor. Assured that he was alone, he turned toward the elevator.

Air hissed behind him. Something sharp pierced his back. He took one stumbling step forward, then the world went dark.

CHAPTER TEN

Mark Tonelli awoke to the feeling of cold linoleum beneath his cheek and a pounding in his head.

"Ah, I see you're finally awake."

Every cell in Mark's body froze at Jamieson's deceptively mild tone.

Damn, damn, damn. The word resonated inside his skull with the rhythm of his headache.

What had he done to give himself away? More important, how was he going to get out of here alive and get back to Faith? The questions gave him something to focus on besides the pain in his head, and the pressure at his wrist and ankles from zip ties.

He had no illusions about Jamieson's plans for him. His hands and feet were bound. Duct tape covered his mouth. Four men stood guard around him in what looked to be a small kitchen, although it was a place Mark had never seen before.

Even though most of his intelligence work was done in restaurants or meeting rooms, Mark had maintained his survival instincts, the ones that had kept him alive on the streets of Moscow as a boy. A good thing, since the hunt for

Nevsky's microchip had put him in more physically dangerous situations these past few months than he'd experienced in years.

Adrenaline pumped through his system, sharpening his mind and heightening his senses. He took note of the distance between him and his guards. Jamieson and one of the guards were the closest to the only door. What he needed to know, but couldn't tell from his position on the floor, was whether or not the guards were normal, or Kaufmann's monsters.

It would be better if—

Jamieson knelt down in front of Mark, extending his palm to reveal Mark's father's little bronze horse. For once, Mark didn't look at the miniature with longing or a burning anger. Instead, he just felt sad.

"You're as much trouble as your father was," Jamieson said conversationally. "I was able to stop your father before he revealed my name to the investigating committee. Don Marrone was more than pleased to order the hit in return for my arranging for certain pending charges to be dropped." He shook his head. "I had hoped your time on the streets of Moscow would wear away all that moral superiority your father instilled in you. Yet here you've betrayed me just as surely as your father."

Mark made an angry sound behind the duct tape. After all these years, he'd finally found the man responsible for his father's death and he was helpless to seek his revenge.

"Unfortunately, you managed to do what your father couldn't. You interfered in my plans." Jamieson rubbed his thumb over the dent in the horse's shoulder. "We discovered your transmissions to the SSU. Tell me, have you been working for the SSU since the beginning? Nod yes or no, please or Victor will break your leg."

Mark shook his head no.

"Strange. I believe you." Jamieson tilted his head to the side. "What turned you? Was it Ivanov?"

Mark nodded.

Jamieson's lips pressed together. "Idiot." His hand closed around the horse, then he straightened out of his crouch.

"You've ruined my plans for you, Mr. Tonelli. You were supposed to be my scapegoat, but only after the anniversary demonstration. Now, with Kaufmann's lab destroyed and the SSU in possession of Kaufmann, I'll be forced to have you killed. Records will show that you'd been embezzling funds in order to support Kaufmann's lab. The investigation will center on you. Meanwhile, the anniversary demonstration will go off as planned. Afterward, Kerberos will remain in high favor. We'll free those scientists currently in custody and then we'll start the lab again using our backup notes."

Jamieson sighed. "It's a pity, Mr. Tonelli. For a while there, I had high hopes for you." He turned to go.

Mark was about to watch his father's murderer walk away and there was nothing he could do about it. Yet oddly enough, he didn't feel bitter. Instead, he felt relieved to know the truth. Revenge didn't matter right now. Getting free and getting to Faith before Jamieson discovered her brother's connection to Kerberos was all that mattered.

Jamieson spoke briefly to the guard by the door, then one of the men accompanied him out of the room.

Leaving Mark and three men.

He tensed. He had a plan, but the only way it was going to work was if he could get someone to take off this damn duct tape. He needed to speak.

But before he could figure out a way to convince one of his guards to cut the tape and let him talk, a boot slammed into his temple and the world went black.

THE NEXT TIME Mark woke up, he was hit by the nauseating stench of diesel fuel and the bone-jarring vibration of tires underneath a corrugated metal floor. Before opening his eyes he flexed his muscles, confirming that his hands and feet were still bound. His mouth, however, was no longer taped.

He cracked open his eyes then immediately shut them again as the faint gray interior of the van he was in spun around him, igniting another headache. He didn't understand why he wasn't dead yet, but he didn't plan on letting this opportunity escape him.

"Don't move," a man's voice said behind him.

Mark flinched. How had he missed that he wasn't alone?

Something sawed through the bindings at his wrists and the thin plastic restraints quickly broke. Mark didn't dare move his arms in case this was some kind of sick game.

"It's okay to move," the man said. "No one in the driver's compartment can see back here." A moment later the restraints at Mark's ankles were cut away.

Mark rolled gingerly to a more comfortable position, then ignored the screaming pain in his head and pushed himself to his knees. "What's going on?" he demanded in a voice gone hoarse.

In the faint light from the rear window Mark recognized one of the men from Jamieson's assassination squads. Not one of the men who'd been in the kitchen.

"Call it an attack of conscience," the man said. "I don't approve of what Jamieson has done with Kerberos, muddying the purity of our mission with those freaky monster men. You were right to help the SSU shut down Kaufmann's down. Now I want you to stop the demonstration."

Mark shook his head, sure he must have misheard. "Excuse me?"

The man nodded toward Mark's hip. "I put a flash drive in your pocket. It has the personnel roster and battle plan for the anniversary attack. Give it to the SSU. Stop Jamieson from killing everyone on that island."

Mark opened his mouth to speak, but the man held up his hand. "I don't have the contacts to get this information acted on immediately. The SSU trusts you. Me and my men will disappear in a few days. We'll tell Jamieson we dumped you in the ocean if he demands proof of your death. By the time he becomes suspicious, your friends at the SSU should have taken care of him for us."

Mark didn't know what to say. He wasn't used to people helping him without asking for something in return. But the man's voice rang with the truth of conviction. So Mark settled for a simple, "Thank you."

"Don't thank me too much," the man said. His teeth flashed white as he smiled. "I still have to make this look good." With that the man opened the back door of the still moving van. Before Mark had any idea what he intended, he found himself picked up and flung toward the side of the road.

Mark had a second to think, "Oh shit, this is going to hurt." Then the ground rose up and smacked him.

Before he passed out yet again, he thought he heard the sound of the man's laughter.

MARK REGAINED consciousness and immediately wished he hadn't. Every part of his body hurt. What—?

Memory came trickling back. Kitchen. Jamieson. Being thrown out of the van.

No wonder he hurt so much.

Driven by the need to get to Faith, Mark climbed gingerly to his feet and took a quick survey of his body. His clothing was torn and he'd landed in a damp, shallow gully next to the road. But his head throbbed only slightly and his vision was clear. He appeared to have suffered mostly cuts and bruises. Good. It would have taken too long to return to the safe house if he had broken bones or a serious concussion.

He felt his pocket. Yes, the flash drive was still there.

He needed to get the data to Ryker. But first he had to figure out where he was and, if possible, get some clean, dry clothes.

Most importantly, he had to return to Faith. He didn't care how secure his safe house was. He wanted Faith under the protection of the SSU before he went after her brother.

Glancing around, Mark wondered which way he should walk. In both directions trees pressed to the edges of the two-lane road. He didn't see any intersecting roads, houses, or even any mailboxes that might give him a clue as to his location. He might as well be in the middle of nowhere.

He thought back, trying to remember the landmarks he'd seen before being thrown out of the van. There. That tree with the dead limb had been on the left, back the way they'd come.

Stepping onto the pavement, Mark began walking.

FAITH PACED AROUND the first floor of the safe house. Mark had been missing for forty-eight hours and she was getting ready to bolt. Best case scenario, he'd fallen critically ill or had an inno-cent accident and was in the hospital, unable to contact her in a secure manner.

Worst case, he'd been taken just like Toby.

Knowing the second option was more likely, Faith should have fled when Mark didn't come home after work that first evening. But she couldn't bear abandoning him. So she'd waited around until the next morning, then donned one of her last disguises and spent the day at a nearby library searching for any mention of Mark in the news. Not finding any reference to him only made her more convinced Jamieson's men had taken him.

Still, she'd snuck back to the safe house that night after

making sure no one was following her. She'd followed the same routine today and from the anxiety knotting her stomach, she was in for another sleepless night.

Knowing she wouldn't do Mark or herself any good if she didn't rest, she went into the downstairs bathroom to grab a glass of water so she could take one of the sleeping pills she occasionally needed.

"Faith!"

Mark's voice sounded so close, Faith screeched and spun around. The glass went flying and shattered against the basin.

"Mark!" He stood at the back door, turning the lock. "Oh, my God, where have you been?" She ran toward him, threw herself into his arms, and plastered his face with kisses. To her shock, he shoved her away.

"Pack your things. We're leaving."

"Wait. What? You vanish for forty-eight hours, show up so suddenly you scare me half to death and expect me to obey your demands?"

He reared back. "Forty-eight hours? I've really been gone that long?"

She nodded. "I've been worried sick." Giving him a quick visual once over, her eyebrows shot up. He looked as if he'd just stepped out of a boxing ring. His face was swollen, bruised and cut. "My God. Mark, what happened? And...are those coveralls you're wearing?"

He scowled and his eyes narrowed. "You haven't seen me for two days and yet you're still here in the safe house? What the hell were you thinking? What if I'd been compromised and gave them this location?"

"I wasn't going to leave you! The only way you had of contacting me was if I stayed put."

"Aggravating woman." Mark stepped forward and kissed her. The kiss was hard and passionate and she could taste blood from his split lip. Still, long before she was ready for it to end she found herself being half-propelled, half-dragged down the hall.

"Mark, what hap—"

"No time." He grabbed her arm. "If you want any chance at saving Toby, you have to leave with me now."

"What's wrong?" she demanded as he tugged her up the stairs. The tension radiating off him scared her.

"Pack your things," Mark ordered. He let go of her arm and nudged her toward the bathroom while he pulled a rolling carry-on suitcase down from the top shelf in the master bedroom. He winced as the case banged his right shoulder on the way down and Faith wondered how many other areas of his body were hurt.

"Mark, what's going on?" Whatever had happened was bad enough that he was ignoring what must be considerable physical pain. Dozens of questions danced across her tongue, but she bit the inside of her cheek and kept silent. Some sixth sense told her he was barely holding onto his control, so she obediently went into the bathroom and starting filling her toiletry case. "What happened that has you dressing like a repairman?" She tried to make her question casual, thinking he'd be more likely to answer if he didn't suspect she was on the verge of freaking out.

"The SSU discovered the location of the lab."

"What? You learned the location of the lab and didn't tell me?" Faith closed her eyes and tried to pretend that this searing pain in her chest wasn't a sense of betrayal.

"No. That's not it." Mark's voice was muffled, and when Faith leaned back so she could see into the bedroom she discovered that he was inside the closet, tossing clothes randomly onto the bed. She winced at the haphazard heap, but she wasn't going to waste time folding things neatly. Picking up on Mark's urgency, she just wanted to get out of here.

With the last piece of clothing freed from the closet, Mark

began shoving items into the suitcase. "No one gave me the location of the lab. The SSU doesn't trust me that much. I've only recently become an ally. Their director, Ryker, called tonight—er—the night I went missing to tell me that Rafe Andros, the SSU agent who'd been one of Kaufmann's victims, finally remembered where he'd been held."

Faith jammed the last of her toiletries into the case.

"Ryker gave me a heads up that the SSU was in the process of launching a raid on the compound. Before I could get out of the building, I was knocked out."

Mark finished stuffing her clothes into her suitcase as she put the toiletry case into her backpack. Her hands shook at the realization of how close she'd come to losing him.

"Ready?" he asked.

She nodded and reached for the backpack, but he shot her one of his patented arrogant looks before swinging the bag over his shoulder. Noticing the way he flinched when the bag's shoulder strap hit his shoulder, Faith slapped his hand away from the suitcase handle. "Stop trying to be Mr. Macho and let me help," she snarled.

Shooting her an annoyed glare, Mark let her take the suitcase and gestured for her to head downstairs.

"You still haven't explained exactly what happened," she said.

"Jamieson had me knocked out and tied up. After admitting he'd ordered my father's death, he gave his men orders to kill me, then left."

Faith gasped and ground to a halt at the bottom of the stairs.

Without looking at her, Mark reached out and grabbed her hand, tugging her forward. "The strange thing was," he said as he snatched their jackets and the bag of prepaid cell phones and headed for the back door, "that I didn't care that much about dying and losing my chance for revenge. My main concern was that I didn't want to leave you."

Filled with tenderness, Faith squeezed his hand. "How'd you escape?"

"I'm lucky," he said. "One of Jamieson's assassins hates what's going on at Kaufmann's lab. He set me free." Mark shook his head. "Then he tossed me out of the back of the van we were in. He said he'd tell Jamieson they'd dumped my body in the ocean."

Faith wanted so badly to hold him. It terrified her that she'd almost lost him and would never have known why. But he was in such a hurry, tossing their bags into the trunk of the car and striding around to the driver's door, that she couldn't allow herself even the small comfort of hugging him.

"My clothes were torn and muddy by the time I made it back to civilization." He attempted a rueful smile as he slid behind the wheel of the car.

Faith kept her mouth shut instead of insisting that she drive.

"These were the only clothes I could find at the time. I stole them out of the back of a truck." He backed the car out of the driveway, then drove at a moderate speed down the road.

"Where are we going?"

"To the SSU." Mark's eyes kept roving from the street to the mirrors, checking for tails. "I bought a prepaid cell phone and called Ryker." Mark smiled as she scoffed. "Yes, I really did go into a convenience store looking like this. Unbelievable, isn't it?"

"There's the arrogance I know and love," she said with a laugh.

Mark sobered. "I love you so much, Faith. I honestly never thought it possible. But I'm so grateful you're in my life."

Faith leaned over and placed a gentle kiss on his bruised cheek. "I love you, too. So, are we driving to the SSU?"

"No. They only have a small administrative office in Washington, D.C. Their main facility, complete with training compound, is in Oregon. That's where we're going. Ryker is going to have a plane waiting for us at a private airstrip about an hour from here."

"Both of us?"

Mark nodded and she nearly sagged with relief. She'd been certain he was going to dump her and go off on his own.

"I can't go back to the office. I'm supposed to be dead. Besides," he dug into the front pocket of the coveralls and pulled out a flash drive. "My rescuer gave me this. He claims it's the battle plans and personnel roster for the upcoming attack. If Toby wasn't picked up in the raid on the lab, then he's probably participating in the attack. The SSU will use the data to try and stop the attack."

Her eyes fixated on the small piece of black plastic. After worrying for so long about her brother, it was almost paralyzing to think her wait might be over. "If Toby is part of the attack team, what are the odds of him coming back alive?"

"The SSU is an honorable group. Their teams will do everything possible to protect your brother."

Faith settled back against the seat, knowing there was no guarantee. In the heat of the moment, or if Toby became aggressive and attacked the SSU soldiers, he might very well be seriously injured or killed. "I'll keep my fingers crossed, then, that he was safely rounded up in the raid."

CHAPTER ELEVEN

Three Days Later
SSU Compound
Oregon

DURING THE FLIGHT to the SSU compound, Faith learned that
Toby had not been one of the men rescued from Dr.
Kaufmann's lab. However, the flash drive provided by Mark's
rescuer confirmed that her brother had been assigned to one of
the Kerberos teams that would be participating in the
upcoming attack.

Her disappointment that Toby remained under Kaufmann's
control was tempered by knowing that most of the men recovered from the lab had been in bad shape. Many of them had
shown significant deterioration of their mental abilities.
Several had physically declined past the point where the side
effects could be reversed.

"What are the chances that you'll be able to return Toby to
normal?" Faith asked Dr. Gabrielle Montague. She and Mark
sat in one of the conference rooms in the main administration

building. Dr. Montague was connected via video link from an SSU plane en route from the facility in Georgia.

"The fact that Toby is capable of participating in the attack means he's still physically and mentally stable," Dr. Montague said. Scratches and bruises marred the skin on her face, and dark circles bagged under her eyes. According to Ryker, Kaufmann had ordered Dr. Montague kidnapped and brought back to his lab. He'd tried to force her to make changes to the drug formula that would eliminate the negative side effects. After being rescued during the SSU's raid, Dr. Montague had thrown herself into trying to find an antidote for the poison that was suspected to be the main weapon in the upcoming attack. She'd also led the effort to reverse the side effects in Kaufmann's victims.

Faith had to admit to being surprised by both the SSU compound and Dr. Montague. The combination training and administrative facility looked like a sprawling college campus set deep in the heart of the Oregon woods, complete with picturesque Victorian style houses, a state-of-the-art medical facility, and even a wildlife rehabilitation center that recovering agents worked at as part of their recovery process.

She'd imagined Dr. Montague as being one of those brilliant women who wore a perpetually distracted look and was socially awkward. Instead, Dr. Montague was an attractive woman with chin length blonde hair, intelligent hazel eyes and an air of both efficiency and compassion.

However, Faith noticed that the doctor's attitude cooled significantly when she talked to Mark. An indication of a long history of bad blood between the SSU and Mark, including a time when he'd left Rafe Andros to die.

"Your brother's prognosis is good if he's brought to us within the next couple of days," Dr. Montague added. "Unfortunately, there's a point past which the mind and body rapidly deteriorate. Based on the timeline you've given me, I suspect your brother is nearing that deadline."

Faith bit her lip, then nodded. So, the urgency in her dreams had been correct.

"I have to warn you," Dr. Montague said. "This video I'm about to show you is from the extensive library of recordings Dr. Kaufmann made regarding his subjects. It contains graphic and disturbing images of violence. Are you certain you want to watch it?"

Faith nodded. She felt Mark's eyes on her but she didn't turn her head. She didn't want to see the worry in his eyes. He'd tried to talk her out of this, but she didn't care if the footage of Dr. Kaufmann's subjects gave her nightmares for years to come. She needed to see for herself what Toby had been put through.

Part of her would rather have Toby be missing than to have him turned into a monster. Because, what if she saw him and instead of feeling sympathy and love she felt fear?

Stop courting heartbreak before it rounds the bend. Just look at the damn video.

Faith straightened her spine. No matter what she learned today, she was resourceful. Strong. She'd take what she learned and make something positive of it.

Mark squeezed her hand, reminding her that she wasn't alone.

"I'm sure," she said firmly.

Dr. Montague pressed her lips together but didn't make any further attempts to change Faith's mind. That made her respect the doctor even more.

Dr. Montague somber gaze met Faith's. "Just let me know when you want me to shut it off. And feel free to jump in with any questions. For people not familiar with the program, some of what you're about to see probably won't make sense." Dr. Montague rubbed her hands up and down her arms. "I've been exposed to at least one of the drugs the men were given intravenously and I can tell you that the burn of the chemicals as they move through your bloodstream is excruciating. I can't imagine what it's like to experience that day after day for weeks on end."

Faith swallowed a lump of fear and gave a thumbs up. As Dr. Montague started the video, Mark put his arm across Faith's shoulders. She reached up and clung to his fingers as horrific images filled the screen.

It didn't do any good to tell herself to just look at faces, scanning for Toby. There was too much pain. Too much desperation, fear and rage. Faith stared in revulsion as the scientists put the men through horrific exercises, testing obedience to orders the men clearly fought against obeying. All the while, the scientists took notes and conferred with one another with clinical detachment. Oblivious to the suffering going on around them.

"We're only holding on to the tapes until we're certain everyone responsible for the program has been punished," Dr. Montague said tightly. "And, of course, we want to make certain that all of the victims have been identified so that their respective agencies can close their investigations and notify any next of kin. The notes you turned over, combined with the data pulled from Kaufmann's lab before it was destroyed should make this a fairly straightforward task."

Watching the violence, and the brutal reactions of the men to the simplest command, Faith prayed that she got to Toby soon. And then she prayed some more that Dr. Montague would be able to restore him.

Faith glanced at the small image of the doctor in the lower right corner of the screen. "Dr. Montague? Are you okay?" The doctor wore the frozen expression of someone enduring past her limit. Still, she gave a curt nod.

That's right, Dr. Montague had been tortured by Dr.

Kaufmann. Not only would the video remind her of her own ordeal, but also of what her lover, Rafe Andros, had suffered.

When the video finally ended, Faith gave a sigh of relief. That had been more difficult to sit through than she'd expected. But necessary. Now she fully understood that Toby might be beyond rational thought when Mark found him. Her brother might not understand language enough to grasp that Mark wanted to help him. Or Toby might have been conditioned to consider every stranger an enemy.

Faith glanced over at Mark, knowing that the plan was for him to leave with the SSU team tonight on their mission to stop the Kerberos men. "How is Mark going to get through to Toby when he finds him?" According to the data recovered from Kaufmann's lab, Toby had not been part of the special group whose members were controllable via a code phrase. Her brother had been trained to respond only to direct orders given in person by his handler.

Dr. Montague rubbed the back of her neck. "That's a good question. You'll have to think of something that serves as a trigger to better memories. With Rafe, it was a scent that we piped into his room." She blushed, and Faith figured the scent must have triggered a memory of their romantic relationship.

Dr. Montague cleared her throat. "I don't think that will work in this case, since Mr. Tonelli will mostly likely be confronting your brother outdoors. I suggest using an audio recording, instead. Is there some silly phrase you used as kids? Maybe a song you used to sing together?"

"Yes. Toby always loved the lullaby our mother sang to us."

"Good. Hopefully, when Mr. Tonelli plays the recording the familiar sounds will stall Toby long enough so Mr. Tonelli can tranquilize him before he attacks."

Faith froze. *Stupid. Stupid.* Her heart had blinded her to so many truths these past few weeks. Why hadn't she realized that Toby might try to kill Mark? She glanced over at him. The thought of her lover fighting for his life against her enraged brother made her vision waver.

Mark must have read her concern in her expression, because he gave her one of his arrogant smiles, then bent his head and gave her a quick kiss. "I'll be fine."

"Mark..." She swallowed. She didn't want to lose him. And yet...she couldn't give up on Toby. No matter how far gone he was, she needed him brought to the SSU, where there was at least a glimmer of a chance he could be cured. How was she supposed to decide between them?

"I'll bring Toby back," Mark said quietly. "I promise. You'll see both of us again."

Out of the corner of her eye Faith saw the video screen go dark as Dr. Montague signed off. "You'd better come back," Faith said fiercely. She gave him a hard kiss of her own. "Because I love you, dammit, and I refuse to lose you."

The SSU's plane would be leaving for the South Pacific in a few hours, but after spending the entire evening in briefings, Mark needed time with Faith.

He cautiously opened the door to their guest apartment, in case she was asleep.

"Mark?" Faith called sleepily from the bedroom. The light went on. "Is that you?"

Relief flooded him at the sound of her voice. Amazing, really, how quickly she'd become his anchor. His solace. Him, Mark Tonelli, the man who didn't care, had become addicted to the loving companionship of a spirited reporter.

"Yes," he called as he slipped out of his shoes and lined them up neatly to the side of the door.

Faith appeared in the bedroom doorway. "How'd the briefing go?"

Mark took a moment to just study her form, backlit by the

bedroom lamp. He felt the familiar tightening of his body as arousal sparked, but also a contented glow. Was this what happily married men experienced every time they were reunited with their wives?

"Mark?" she prompted.

"The briefing went well. Once upon a time I'd have disparaged their skills, but the truth is, Ryker's assembled a highly efficient and extremely capable group of men and women. I'm not a military planner, but it seems they've prepared for every contingency."

"It's clear that they're not to harm Toby?"

Mark crossed the living room and took her in his arms. "Yes. Everyone has seen his photo. I'm confident he won't be harmed unnecessarily."

He saw the shadow cross her face. "Faith, you—"

She placed a quick kiss on his mouth. "I know. If Toby attacks and can't be safely tranq'd, then the SSU agents might be forced to fight him and he could be hurt. I don't like it, but I understand."

Mark inhaled, catching Faith's sugar-cookie-and-cinnamon scent mingled with unfamiliar honeysuckle that must have come from the body lotion the SSU had stocked in the bathroom. "I'm proud of the way you're handling this, Faith."

She gave a shaky laugh that made him tighten his arms around her. "You wouldn't say that if you knew how scared and disturbed I feel. Before you came in, I'd been lying in bed for a couple of hours, desperately trying to sleep, but I couldn't stop thinking about the images from the video. I—" She shuddered.

"Violence isn't new to me. I've covered wars, riots, and massacres, although my focus was always on the people involved and on discovering the hidden injustices that accompanied such encounters. After the first few assignments I learned how to compartmentalize my emotions. How to burn off stress and to use meditation to calm my mind before sleep so the chance of having a nightmare was reduced."

"I hate the idea of you experiencing nightmares," Mark murmured.

There was that unfamiliar protective streak again, but he didn't care. When Faith hurt, he hurt.

"Thank you. While I wasn't nearly as jaded as many of my fellow investigative journalists, I thought I had a fairly broad idea of the types of atrocities human beings committed against one other. But Mark—" Her words choked off on a slight sob.

He found himself making nonsense soothing noises and stroking his hands gently over her back.

"Mark, what we saw on those videos was wrong on a fundamental level."

"I know."

"That's right, you'd already seen similar activities at Ivanov's lab, hadn't you?"

"Yes, and they continue to bother me to this day."

Faith snuggled against him. "Yeah, I have a feeling the images from Kaufmann's videos will be starring in my nightmares for years to come. But before you say 'I told you so' let me remind you that it was my choice. If I'm going to help Toby heal, then I needed to understand what he's been through. No matter how horrific the images."

She raised her tear-drenched face to his. "I'm so scared that you and Toby will face one another and one of you will end up seriously injured. Or dead." Her voice caught. "Please be careful. I don't want to lose either you or Toby."

Mark's heart swelled. Since his mother and stepfather had died, no one had given a damn about him until Faith. His previous lovers had only been concerned about short-term pleasure. He wasn't even certain if they'd liked him. But Faith knew the worst of him and still loved him. Would fight for both him and her brother, no matter the risk to herself. "You are one brave lady, you know that?"

"Naw. I'm just too stubborn to do what's safest."

Mark stepped back so he could look her in the eyes. "No, Faith. You're loyal. You love deeply enough to ignore the risk to yourself in order to help your brother and to keep going even when most women would have been scared off. That's courage."

Faith reached up and touched his cheek. "You're wrong. The love between brother and sister is strong enough that I'm sure you could find plenty of women who wouldn't give up. I—"

Mark leaned down and gave her a quick, hard kiss. "Why are we talking, Faith? I have to leave in a couple of hours."

Knowing how much she loved it, he bent and scooped her into his arms, grinning at her delighted shriek as he carried her into the bedroom. Humbled by the fact that this amazing woman loved him, he laid Faith gently on the bed. The lamplight bathed her body in a soft glow.

"Come here, Mark." She gave him a seductress's smile and held out her arms.

Buoyed by something he thought might be joy, he lowered himself to the bed and proceeded to show her once again how much he loved her.

CHAPTER TWELVE

The Next Day
Washraiti Island, Salaqut

MARK KNEW that Faith had changed him on a fundamental level when he stepped off the plane on Washraiti Island without a complaint on his lips. Oh, he noticed the humidity, the stench of the jungle, and the bugs that swarmed him on the short journey from the plane to the Jeep, but for once his first thought wasn't disgust. Instead, he was filled with anticipation of the upcoming confrontation. Two of his primary goals were about to be accomplished. First, the information he'd provided Ryker had led both to this assault and to the SSU taking action back in the States that would land Jamieson in jail. It wasn't the direct revenge that he'd longed for, but given the circumstances, it was enough.

More importantly, he was about to rescue Toby, making Faith happy. He'd never have believed it possible to fall so deeply in love so quickly, particularly not so soon after his ill-timed infatuation with Susana Dias. But he had.

He'd been hurt when Susana fell for SSU agent Kai

Paterson, the man who'd reached her before Mark. Now, though, he owed the man a debt of gratitude. What he'd felt for Susana had been just a shiver of emotion. His feelings for Faith were an earthquake.

As he settled into his assigned mobile housing unit, he smiled despite the spartan accommodations. Since he'd started chasing Nevsky's microchip he'd been in the jungle more times than he cared to count. Complaining all the way. Yet today he'd eagerly entered the jungle. Because, for the first time in years, someone else's happiness was more important than his own.

Thinking back, he was grateful for his visit to Ivanov's lab. That trip had opened his eyes, revived his underutilized conscience, and brought to life unfamiliar feelings of empathy. It had started the softening of his harsh attitude toward other people, making him receptive to the connection he'd forged with Faith.

As strange as it sometimes felt to care about another person, he liked the man he was when he was with her.

He sighed. Even knowing he was heading out on a mission to help her, it had been incredibly difficult to leave Faith last night. She'd been curled against him in bed and Mark had hated to leave her warmth. She'd been so exhausted, she'd barely stirred when he kissed her lightly and slid out of bed. Then he'd stood there for a long time, just watching her sleep. Experiencing an unfamiliar peace. He'd felt as if she belonged in his bed not just for a night, but for always. Which made no sense. He'd never wanted a wife or children. Yet the idea of marrying Faith wouldn't leave him alone.

So this is love, he'd thought. *I like it.*

Finally, he'd shaken himself out of his daze, stepped away from their bed and headed into the shower. He shouldn't have bothered. After two minutes in this humidity he'd been drenched with sweat. He glanced down at the jungle fatigues he wore and grinned. At least he wasn't ruining one of his prized suits.

The SSU soldiers hadn't wanted him along and had voiced their disapproval when he'd been given a uniform. Many of them looked at him with animosity, no doubt having heard how he'd left Rafe Andros to die on the tarmac in Cozumel. At the time, Mark had been in a desperate race to get to a man who could provide the location of Dr. Nevsky's microchip. Rafe had been bleeding from a gunshot wound when Mark found him at the airstrip. Mark had convinced Rafe to reveal the address where the other Andros brother, Niko, was headed to meet the informant. With that information obtained, Rafe had become nothing but an inconvenience, so Mark had walked away.

Mark didn't blame the SSU agents for viewing him as an enemy. Yes, Ryker had explained that Mark was only along to help retrieve Toby. But it would take more than words for them to trust him.

No matter. He didn't need their trust, just to be left alone. Luckily, the notes on the flash drive contained details on Toby's mission and staging point, so Mark wouldn't have to go chasing all over the island. Instead, he'd accompany the SSU's team, wait until Kaufmann's teams were subdued, then search among the defeated men for Toby.

Every SSU agent had been shown Toby's picture. Yet no one could guarantee that in the flurry of battle Toby would be recognized and left alone. All Mark could do was stay alert and be ready to intervene on Toby's behalf if necessary.

Because there were too many variables for Mark to control in this situation, he'd found himself increasingly relying on hope. Another foreign emotion.

Shaking his head, he pushed open the door to the housing unit and stepped out into the humidity. It was nearly time for the assault to begin.

Even as he swatted at mosquitoes, his lips twitched into a grin as adrenaline hit his system. He felt a stronger rush knowing he was about to enter a possibly physically dangerous situation than he experienced when arranging for a hostile takeover of a criminal's businesses. A sensation similar to the heightened awareness he remembered from his days of thievery on the streets of Moscow.

He could definitely understand why field operators became addicted to this thrill.

"You almost done there?"

Faith startled as Daniel Lang, one of the SSU's research specialists, stopped in the doorway of the tiny office she'd been given. "Sorry," she mumbled, glad that her laptop's screen was turned away from the door, hiding her work. "Guess I'm a bit jumpy."

Daniel nodded. "Understandable. It's your brother over there."

She shrugged, letting him believe that was the main reason she was on edge. Yes, she was worried sick that the attack would result in Toby's death. Or Mark's. Still, she'd been managing pretty well to compartmentalize her fear so that she could work. The truth of why her nerves were stretched resided on her laptop.

"So, are you finished?" Daniel asked.

"Uh, yeah." Making sure he couldn't see her screen, she brought up the spreadsheet she'd been working on. Ryker had assigned her to help match the names of the men targeted by Jamieson as potential Kerberos subjects to those men the SSU had recovered from Kaufmann's lab. Not all of the men were capable of communicating their names, so Faith used the detailed catalog Mark had helped put together in order to compare physical descriptions.

Daniel worked on verifying which men were dead. Once they finished identifying the victims, the SSU would reach out to the appropriate authorities so that the family members could be notified of their loved ones' status.

Another team would try to track down the remaining men on the Kerberos list who the SSU had not yet located.

Faith sent her list to the printer. "There you go."

Daniel picked up the multi-page document. "Great. Thanks. I'll shoot you another list of names in a bit. Why don't you take a break for now?"

Faith gave him a vague smile and a nod, her tension not ebbing until he'd headed down the hallway toward his own office.

Damn, that had been close. Faith got up and shut her office door, taking a risk and locking it as well. She hoped no one would bother her for a few more minutes. That's all she needed to finish going through the file on Dr. Mikhail Nevsky.

She couldn't decide whether the security on the SSU's internal server was lax because the external security was so tight, or whether someone on the research team actually wanted her to poke her nose into areas that she wasn't authorized to view. Nevertheless, Faith was running with the opportunity.

Maybe another woman would feel guilty over repaying Ryker's hospitality and his assistance with finding her brother by preparing an exposé on the decades of experimental research that had led to Dr. Kaufmann's program. But Faith felt a driving need to understand every aspect of the program that had disrupted her brother's life.

Unfortunately, the more she dug into the SSU's files, the more history she uncovered. According to the records she'd reviewed, the United States government had been experimenting with ways of using chemicals to enhance soldiers since the Vietnam War. Certain side effects such as insane rages had been documented during the war. Despite official declarations to the contrary, the experiments had continued in various forms. The most recent being Dr. Kaufmann's program.

Faith's stomach cramped thinking about all the men who'd suffered under the government sanctioned programs. If, after Toby was rescued, there was no public disclosure of what had happened, she would take her findings public. Her lips curled. Siobahn would love to sink her teeth into this. Together they'd write a series of articles that would shine so much light on the experiments that the government wouldn't dare restart them.

Faith downloaded another set of files onto her flash drive. Then, figuring she'd pushed her luck as far as she could for the day, she unlocked her door. Several minutes later, she received her next list of names and once again began the slow, heartbreaking process of cross-checking victims.

Washraiti Island, Salaqut

MARK COULDN'T BELIEVE his luck. He'd found Toby Andrews. For some reason, the man had broken away from his assigned group. Now Toby crashed through the jungle a few yards ahead of Mark, making animal sounds of panic.

Mark didn't know what had scared Faith's brother, but at least his trail was easy to follow. Plus, the dense vegetation slowed Toby down enough for Mark to keep up with him, even with Toby's enhanced speed.

Mark had already radioed the SSU team, letting them know he was in pursuit. To his surprise, no one from the Kerberos team had come after Toby. Perhaps they were too close to the launch of their attack to waste time on an unstable man who couldn't stop them.

Toby tripped on an exposed root and nearly went down.

"Stop, Toby Andrews," Mark said in a loud, clear voice of command. "I have a message from your sister. From Faith."

The man growled and turned around. Even though Dr. Montague had warned Mark to expect rage and madness, he wasn't prepared for the feral, assessing look Toby gave him.

He fought the urge to back up. "Treat him like a wild animal," Dr. Montague had warned during their final briefing. "Stay calm and don't make any threatening moves. His handler is the only one he's supposed to listen to. Depending on what phase he's in, he may or may not be receptive to your conversation. Most likely you'll have to sedate him."

Mark carried the tranquilizer gun the SSU had issued him, but he'd promised Faith he'd only use it as a last resort.

Wetting his dry lips, Mark stared into Toby's eyes. "Faith misses you," he said.

Toby winced. His hands went to his temples. "Faith...bad," he groaned. "Kill...Faith...kill...all."

Mark shook his head. "No. Faith loves you. Kaufmann lied to you. Kaufmann is bad. Listen." He pulled the voice recorder out of his pocket and pushed play.

A sweet lullaby in Faith's crystal clear voice poured out of the recorder. Toby's head jerked back as if someone had yanked on a cord around his neck. His hands dropped to his sides and he glanced around fearfully.

"No," he moaned.

Mark turned up the volume. He was still amazed that Faith had such a beautiful singing voice. But the effect of her voice on him was immediate. Mark forgot the heat and the dirt and the bugs. He only remembered Faith. Her smile. The way her eyes shone with confidence and trust when she looked at him. The small, contented sigh she'd given him after they'd made love last night.

For her sake, he hoped this worked. It would break her heart if he didn't bring her brother back. Yet he also didn't want

Faith to see this wild man who'd dropped to his knees as if his sister's melodic notes were nails being driven into his flesh.

Toby's hands went back up to his head. He yanked on his hair. "Stop!" he shouted. "No more! Hurts." His face twisted, contorting into an expression of such deep pain that Mark had to turn away.

The sound of repeated thudding made Mark look back. Toby was banging his head against the ground. "Stop...love...obey...hurts...kill...sleep..." The man sobbed each word in the pauses between slamming his head against the earth.

"Toby, stop!" Dr. Montague had warned Mark that any attempt to expose Toby to his past would conflict with Kaufmann's conditioning, result in excruciating headaches and possibly make Toby try to kill whoever had brought up the memory.

Mark shut off the recorder, figuring that if Toby hadn't attacked him yet he wasn't going to. "I can help you."

Toby lay quietly with his forehead resting on the ground. Still, Mark watched him warily, all too aware of the enhanced speed at which the man could attack him.

"Do you understand me?" Mark demanded. "I can take you to someone who will make the headaches stop. Who will get rid of the voices. Give you control of your mind again. Reunite you with Faith." Dr. Montague had promised she'd do everything she could to restore Toby to his previous self.

Mark prayed that Toby wasn't too far gone to make a full recovery.

"Toby! Answer me."

Toby lifted his head. His lips curled back and he snarled at Mark, snapping his teeth like a rabid dog. He rose into a crouch and his powerful body tensed, ready to leap.

A woman's scream lanced through the thick jungle air.

Toby jumped to his feet. "Faith!" he yelled, charging into the jungle.

"No! Toby wait. Faith's not here. She's safe. She's—" But Toby was gone.

Cursing under his breath, Mark shoved the recorder in his pocket and took off after him.

MARK FOLLOWED Toby into a clearing and pulled up short at what he saw. Shit. The bodies of four guards lay scattered around a truck that must be one of the SSU's mobile labs. Two of the men had broken necks. One had multiple stab wounds and a slit throat. The other man looked as if he'd been beaten repeatedly with a blunt object about the head and chest. Despite the damage he'd suffered, he was trying to pull himself toward the truck.

Mark threw a quick glance to where Toby had disappeared through the twisted door to the lab, then hurried over to the man. "What happened?"

"Kaufmann's men...two...caught us by...surprise...wear...ing...protective suits...tranq darts...bullets...bounce off..." His eyes turned toward Mark, pleading. "Help...Dr...Mon...tague..." He coughed violently, then collapsed.

Mark bolted toward the lab. If the men killed Dr. Montague, then who would return Toby to normal? How would he explain to Faith that he'd failed her?

Mark jumped over the mangled ruin of the door and into an antechamber that must have been the security command center. Broken monitors littered the floor. A chair stuck out of the far wall. All that remained of the observation window were jagged pieces of glass and fragments of wire.

Beyond that, a growing pool of blood seeped out from under the body of another guard. Dr. Montague lay in a boneless heap at the foot of a supply cabinet. One of Kaufmann's men kicked Dr. Montague repeatedly in the face and torso while a second man smashed beakers and shoved everything from the countertops onto the floor.

The man attacking Dr. Montague threw back his head, yelled in primal fury, and pulled a knife from his belt.

With an answering bellow, Toby charged the man. The pair went down in a tangle of flying fists.

The other attacker was too busy trying to pry a cabinet off the wall to notice the fight. But Mark knew it would only be a matter of time.

The man's hood had slipped off his head, leaving the back of his neck exposed. Mark raised his pistol and fired just as the cabinet broke free of the wall. Kaufmann's man staggered back under its weight. Mark fired repeatedly until the man landed on his back under the weight of the cabinet.

Satisfied that the man was dead, Mark turned in time to see Kaufmann's man kick Toby in the stomach. Toby landed on his back with a grunt.

Kaufmann's man ignored Toby and rushed over to Dr. Montague. Dropping to his knees, he raised his knife and plunged it into her chest.

"No!" Toby struggled to sit up, reaching out as if he would choke the man. Tears streamed down his cheeks as his mouth twisted in horror. "No hurt Faith!"

Shit. Dr. Montague was roughly the same size as Faith, and with her straight blonde hair hidden under a protective cap, Toby wouldn't realize this wasn't his curly-haired sister. He must have thought Faith was close by because of the voice recording Mark had played for him.

The man yanked the knife out of Dr. Montague.

A second later, Rafe Andros dove through the window and tackled the man.

Mark sensed another man heading toward Toby and he threw himself at Faith's brother, pushing Toby to the floor and shielding him with his own body. "Jurassic Park," Mark said, giving the code word to indicate he was friendly. "Don't hurt this one. This is Toby. I—" A wave of pain bit off the rest of his sentence.

Kaufmann's man yanked his knife free of Mark's lower back as he and Andros rolled away.

Mark's vision tunneled. "Don't...hurt...Toby..." he gasped. Then he lost consciousness.

IAN MCDERMOTT, Ryker's administrative assistant, was at the door when Faith answered the knock at her guest apartment at four in the morning. Swallowing her dread, she forced herself to meet his somber eyes. "What's happened? Are Toby and Mark all right?"

"Your brother is okay. But, I'm sorry, ma'am. Mr. Tonelli was injured during the attack."

Faith swayed and gripped the doorframe to keep herself upright. No. Not Mark. Please, no. "How bad is it?" She had to force the words out of her parched mouth.

McDermott glanced up and down the hallway. "I think it would be better for me to tell you inside, ma'am."

"Oh. Yes. Of course." Faith shuffled out of the way so the man could enter and tried to use the action of closing the door to ground herself. No matter what McDermott had to say, Mark wasn't dead. She had to hold on to that thought or go crazy.

"Tell me," she demanded. "What happened?"

"While trying to protect your brother during a fight with Kaufmann's enhanced men, Mr. Tonelli was stabbed in the lower back. The knife did severe damage to his internal organs. He's being medevaced to a surgical trauma center."

Oh, God. She crossed her arms over her chest. "Do they expect him to live?"

"It's touch and go right now, ma'am."

"I want transport to the hospital. I need to see him."

"Yes, ma'am. That's why I'm here."

"Good. Just let me change and we can go." She headed toward the bedroom, calling back, "What about Toby?"

"Your brother is a bit beat up, but sustained no serious injuries."

"Oh, thank God."

"He's en route to our Georgia lab. Our medical team has given him starting doses of the drugs that will help calm his rage and bring his intellect back online. The team reports that he's resting quietly."

Faith's shoulders sagged in relief.

"Unfortunately, Dr. Montague was also...um...injured in the attack."

Faith paused and turned around. "What the hell does that mean?"

"Ah...apparently she died for a few minutes," McDermott said. "But Kai Paterson figured out that administering a specific drug would revive her. She's now in a coma."

Faith's stomach twisted into a complex knot of tension. "God, poor Rafe." She'd never met the man, but she'd heard the story about his recovery and how his love for Dr. Montague had been the only thing that kept him going. It was too cruel for Rafe to be on the brink of losing the woman he loved on top of everything he'd endured at the hands of Dr. Kaufmann.

"Will this impact Toby's progress?"

"No. Paterson is Dr. Montague's co-leader on the medical team, so he'll be taking charge of your brother's recovery. Paterson and the rest of the team are extremely knowledgeable and skilled.Your brother's progress should not be affected in the least by Dr. Montague's absence."

"Is it—" She cleared her throat. "Would it be possible to see Toby before he reaches Georgia? Just to ease my mind?"

McDermott glanced down at his phone. "If we leave within the next three minutes we should be able to meet his plane as it lands here. You won't have much time, though. He's going to be transferred immediately to another plane."

"Done." Faith raced into the bedroom, threw on some clothes, and was out the door with McDermott with a minute to spare. "After Toby, you'll take me to Mark?"

"Yes."

To Faith's relief, they reached the small airport not far from the SSU compound in time to watch the transport plane land. Lips pressed tightly together, she watched as the plane was secured and stairs were pushed up to the plane's door. A few agonizingly long moments later, two guards appeared, escorting Toby between them.

Tears stung her eyes. Toby was confined in a straightjacket, and his face was covered with bruises, but he held his head high and walked without limping. Best of all, his expression was wary, not angry.

Halfway to the second plane, Toby noticed Faith standing off to the side. His dark blue eyes lit up.

"Faith okay?" he shouted.

She nodded, then forced a verbal response through her tears-clogged throat. "I'm fine, Toby."

Despite her reassurance, Toby tried to get away from his guards, who struggled to restrain him. "No! Toby don't fight them. I'm coming."

Faith rushed over, careful to stop before she got within striking distance. "Let these men help you, Toby. They're taking you to some very good doctors. They're going to make you better."

"Faith come?"

She shook her head. "Not yet. A...friend...of mine is hurt. I need to be with him. But I'll see you soon, okay?"

"No. Want Faith. Miss Faith."

"I know, Toby. I miss you, too. But the SSU is going to help you. I promise. We'll get to visit again once you're better."

"Nooo..."

It took all of Faith's willpower to walk away from Toby's lost puppy eyes and tune out his cries of protest. She was surprised that he'd reacted positively to seeing her. Before the attack, Dr. Montague had warned that Kaufmann used torture and drugs to turns his victims against their family and friends. So Faith had expected Toby to treat her like an enemy. Maybe even strike out at her.

That he'd wanted the comfort of her presence made it that much harder to leave him.

Returning to McDermott, she nodded. "Let's go." She had to get out of here before she did something really stupid, like run back to Toby and insist on going with him. There was nothing she could do to help her brother. But she could make damn sure Mark knew he wasn't alone. That he had a reason to fight for his life.

She loved him, and she wasn't going to let him forget it.

CHAPTER THIRTEEN

Three Days Later
SSU Medical Facility
Oregon

MARK STARED IMPATIENTLY at the door of his hospital room. Faith had promised to return this afternoon at two, and it was four past. While he understood that Faith was being kept busy by the SSU as they tied up the loose ends from the aborted attack, he didn't rest easy without her. Forget pain medication. Having Faith by his side was all he needed.

He almost scoffed at such sappy thoughts, but her love filled him so completely there was little room for pain. She softened the edges of the arrogant, self-centered man he'd become during his quest for revenge and turned him into a more patient, more compassionate man. The fact that he hadn't once asked for an update on Jamieson and Kerberos was proof of how much he'd changed. Right now he was more concerned about Toby's progress, because that had the greatest potential to hurt Faith.

He hoped Dr. Montague had survived. He liked the woman

and knew that she would fight for Faith's brother. But last he heard, the doctor was still in a coma.

Six after the hour and still no Faith. Mark scowled and thought about ringing for the nurse.

You're acting like a petulant boy.

He sighed and tried to curb his impatience. If only he could get out of this damn bed and pace, maybe he'd be able to rid himself of some of this nervous energy. Instead, he had so many tubes running into him he felt like a science experiment. He knew he was lucky to be alive, but he was tired of having his bodily functions performed by machines. He wanted out of here.

He wanted Faith, dammit.

Five minutes later, the door finally opened, but it wasn't Faith. A lean man about six feet tall with a thin, aristocratic face and piercing gray eyes walked in, moving with the easy confidence of a natural born leader. Ryker. Mark tried not to let his disappointment show, but he must have given himself away. Ryker gave him a knowing smile.

"Don't worry, Faith is out in the waiting room. I asked her to let me speak to you alone first." Ryker set a digital voice recorder down on the bedside table and turned it on.

"Vincente Tonelli was trouble," Jamieson's voice said coldly.

Mark glanced at Ryker in surprise. He'd never mentioned that Jamieson had arranged his father's death. How had Ryker known?

"It was only a minor case," Jamieson's voice continued. "A former soldier, listed as dead, had been found unconscious in a ditch and been brought to the local VA hospital. When the man awoke he went crazy, killing everyone within reach before the security team tranquilized him." Jamieson's voice dripped with scorn.

"It should have been a simple case. The man was guilty. He should have been convicted and locked up. Then we would have been able to arrange for a quiet assassination away from the public eye. But Tonelli believed the man's story of a secret government program and drugs that made him insane with rage. Tonelli started his own investigation. We couldn't allow that. So we arranged for him to be killed by Don Marrone's men, and set it up so that all evidence pointed back to a mob case Tonelli had recently presided over."

Mark closed his eyes. He'd known Jamieson was guilty, but hearing the details that led to his father's death hurt more than he'd expected.

Jamieson's voice continued, explaining how he'd kept an eye on Mark and eventually decided to use his desire for retribution against him. Finally, just when Mark couldn't stand listening any more, Ryker shut off the recorder and returned it to his pocket.

"What's going to happen to Jamieson?" Mark asked.

"He's in federal custody," Ryker said. "Once we're satisfied that we've rounded up all of his spies and put an end to Kerberos, he'll go on trial."

"And President MacAdam?"

A touch of regret or sadness passed across Ryker's face. "His attorney was pushing for him to be declared insane, but MacAdam took offense and fired him. He's still insisting it was his right as Commander In Chief to attack the terrorists in the manner he saw fit."

"Mass murder." The phrase made Mark slightly ill. He'd worked for Kerberos. Enjoyed the freedom it had allowed him. He'd had no qualms about the selective killing of individuals who threatened his country. The murder of thousands of innocents was another story. He hated to think how close he'd come to being an unknowing accomplice.

Ryker nodded. "Thank you for helping us stop them. I believe we're square now."

Mark felt some of the tension ease out of him. Ryker might

suspect he'd killed Marrone, but he wasn't going to pursue it. And Ryker was apparently willing to forget about the harm he'd caused the SSU.

"You're welcome," Mark said.

Ryker glanced toward the door and smiled. "I'd better leave now, before your lady has me thrown out. Good luck."

"One more thing."

Ryker raised one brow.

"I want to tell Faith everything," Mark said. "She deserves to know."

"She's a reporter. For the protection of everyone involved, I'll need a statement in writing promising that she won't take the classified material she's been exposed to and make it public without receiving authorization from myself and the various agencies involved."

From Ryker's quick response, Mark knew that the SSU director had already anticipated his request. "I'll tell her that."

"Very well."

Mark watched Ryker leave with a twinge of regret. If his life had gone differently, if he hadn't been warped by his need for justice and his sense of entitlement, he would have liked to work for a man as honest and trustworthy as Ryker. Rafe Andros and the others at the SSU were very lucky people.

Mark sighed and closed his eyes. Truth was, he was finished with this spying business. He wanted peace. To settle down with Faith. Maybe start an import business, bringing in luxury goods from Russia and the former Soviet bloc. He still had plenty of contacts.

He gave a rueful smile. Or maybe not. Too many of those contacts skirted the edge of the law. He was done with that. He didn't want danger. He wanted a quiet life with the woman he loved.

Seven Weeks Later
SSU Laboratories
Georgia

FAITH STOOD ALONE in the small, unfurnished room, waiting anxiously for Toby to be brought in. Since his rescue, she'd only been allowed to see Toby that one time on the tarmac. But Dr. Montague, now back to work and in charge of Toby's care, had just contacted Faith to let her know that Toby was stable enough to meet his sister again.

Faith's stomach danced nervously. How would her brother have changed? Would he be angry that she'd left him alone with the SSU? Did he realize the scope of the attack that had almost taken place?

A part of Faith still couldn't believe what she'd learned. The President of the United States had been prepared to decimate an entire population in an attempt to ease his pain over the murder of his five-year-old son. If the attack had succeeded, Toby would have been an accomplice, no matter how unwilling.

Thank God for the SSU. Knowing her brother was almost back to normal eased the sting of having to promise in writing not to reveal any of the details of the attack, Kerberos, or Kaufmann's program. To the rest of the country, the President had resigned due to sudden health reasons, and his undisclosed diagnosis was also blamed for his recent death. Beyond Siobahn's initial article, there'd been no additional mention in the press of the missing service personnel or any hint of the experiments being run.

Because Ryker believed that not all the guilty parties had been discovered, Faith had warned Siobahn to keep her head down and to stay away from anything remotely related to the situation. Perhaps someday they'd be allowed to write the story. Just not now.

For Toby's sake, Faith didn't mind putting a temporary cap on it.

A knock sounded on the door, then one of the guards stepped into the room. He raised an eyebrow at Faith. She nodded, while her stomach turned cartwheels.

Toby entered a second later. As a precaution, the two guards stayed just inside the door. But Faith didn't care. All her attention was on her brother.

He was slightly more muscular than she'd remembered. Lines of strain on his face made him look older and she hoped that the haunted edge to his eyes would eventually go away.

What mattered most, though, was his smile. It lit up his face and chased away the shadows. "Faith!" He held open his arms and she rushed into his embrace.

"Oh, God, Toby, I've missed you so much. How are you? Are you in any pain? Can you—"

"Hush," Toby ordered. He held her tightly and his cheek pressed against the top of her head. "I'm okay, sis. Not quite fully normal, but almost. Dr. Montague and her team are miracle workers."

Faith smiled up at him through tears of joy and relief. "I was so afraid…"

He nodded and she saw his eyes dampen. "I was, too. But everything is going to be okay. I expect to be released next week. So," he cleared his throat. "Tell me about you."

"Oh Toby, it's the most amazing thing. I'm in love…"

Six Weeks Later
Maryland

"THIS IS STUPID." Faith paced back and forth in the living room of the temporary apartment she and Mark had rented not far from the Maryland schools where Faith had resumed teaching.

"I love you. You love me. Toby's my brother, not some sort of feudal lord who gets to decide who I marry." She threw a glare at Mark as she passed him. To her great annoyance, he looked completely unruffled. Normally, when he was in fully polished GQ mode she wanted nothing more than to mess him up. Today, though, it pissed her off that he could remain so calm when he was about to meet Toby for the first time since her brother had regained his faculties.

God, she owed so much to Dr. Montague and her team. Toby's recovery had gone smoothly. Faith had been in frequent contact with him these past few weeks as he finished the last of his treatments and adjusted to being in the real world. He'd even completed an assignment for the SSU.

He was back to being the overbearing, always-got-your-back brother she remembered, so she didn't know why she was so nervous. Toby's temper was under control. Yes, he'd always been aggressive toward her boyfriends, but Mark wasn't the type to cut and run. So why this tangle of knots in her belly?

"Relax, Faith," Mark soothed. "I'm not going to abandon you if Toby decides he doesn't like me. But he is the head of your family. It's only polite to ask him for your hand in marriage."

She threw her hands up in the air. "It's archaic, that's what it is. As if I can't make up my own damn mind."

This time as she neared Mark, he stepped into her path and took gentle hold of her upper arms. "Faith, what's really bothering you? I've never seen you so anxious before."

"Ha. That's because you were off rescuing Toby and nearly *dying* and so you missed my near panic attack when I received the news that you'd been hurt."

Mark winced.

"I'm sorry," she added hastily. "That was uncalled for."

"But true."

"Well—"

He shook his head. "You're never going to let me live that down, are you?"

She managed a weak smile. "Probably not."

Mark brushed a kiss across her lips. "Tell me what's wrong, Faith."

She sighed and stepped into his embrace. "I'm scared that Toby won't like you."

Mark gave her a gentle squeeze. "You already told him of my involvement with Jamieson and Kerberos and he hasn't told you to stop seeing me, right?"

"Right."

"So quit worrying. If we don't get along, we'll deal with the tension the best we can. I'll say it again, I'm marrying you with or without his consent. But given what he's been through, I thought he deserved the respect of having me ask for your hand in marriage."

"You're so old-fashioned, you know that?"

She felt a kiss on her hair. "Yes. But you love me anyway."

He sounded so smug, it would do him good for her to deny it. Keep his ego in check. But she couldn't lie to him. "Yeah," she said, snuggling against him. "I do."

"I—"

The doorbell rang.

Faith pushed away from Mark. "Oh, God, he's here. How do I look?" She reached up and touched her hair.

"Shh. You look beautiful as always." He gave her a smile warm with love and reassurance. "Faith, he's your brother. He's seen you at your worst and Lord knows you've seen him at his worst."

"I know. But it will tear me apart if you two don't get along. I want you both in my life." She fiddled with Mark's perfectly aligned necktie.

The bell rang again and Faith could picture her brother's

annoyed face. "Coming!" She raced to the door and flung it open.

"Toby!" Her brother looked years younger than when she'd last seen him. He would always carry a bit of extra muscle because of Kaufmann's designer steroids, but overall Toby appeared the same fit, dark haired older brother she loved.

He grinned at her and the skin around his dark blue eyes crinkled. "Hey, Faith." Then he pulled her into a bear hug and swung her around.

"Toby, put me down or I'm gonna puke!"

He nearly dropped her. "What's wrong? Are you sick?" His eyes widened. "Shit, Tonelli hasn't gotten you pregnant already, has he?"

"No." She laughed shrilly, silently cursing the nerves that had turned her into a ninny. "Of course not. I just..." She glanced back over her shoulder and saw Mark standing patiently by the sofa. Turning back around, she met Toby's worried eyes. "I just really, really want you two to like each other."

"She's been a nervous wreck," Mark added, coming up beside her and putting one arm around her waist. He held out his hand. "Mark Tonelli. I'm pleased to meet you again under better circumstances."

Toby sized Mark up before shaking hands. "Toby Andrews. I remember you. You played me a tape of Faith singing."

"That's right."

"Thanks for coming to get me, and for keeping Faith safe from Jamieson and his men."

Mark shook his head. "Your sister was doing an excellent job of evasion without me, something I understand is mostly due to the extensive training you gave her. Which means I should be thanking you." He stepped back. "Please, come in."

Toby nodded at Mark, then gave Faith a wink as he passed by. "He'll do," her brother murmured.

All the tension that had been riding her these past weeks seeped right out of Faith, leaving her legs wobbly.

"Easy there," Mark whispered, tightening his arm around her as they followed Toby into the living room. "I've got you."

She grinned up at him, finally accepting that everything was going to be okay. "I know. Now and for always."

DEAR READER

Thank you for spending time with Mark and Faith. I hope you enjoyed reading *Payback* as much as I enjoyed writing it!

I never intended for Mark to get his own book. He was supposed to die at the end of *Retribution*, sacrificing his own life to save Gabby. But no, he had to go and fall in love with Faith! And well, I pretty much always do what my characters tell me. So *Payback* was born. However, I'd had so much fun writing Mark as a jerk, that I wasn't sure if I'd be able to treat him as a hero. He surprised me. Faith really had an amazing effect on him.

Finally, if you enjoyed reading *Payback*, please consider recommending it to family, friends, and anyone else you think might be interested in Mark and Faith's adventures. Leaving a review on the retail store where you purchased it or on Goodreads will also help other readers discover *Payback*.

Thank you for your support!

If you'd like to learn more about Siobahn Murphy, the woman who captures Ryker's heart, pick up *Aftermath*, the fifth book in the SSU series.

Happy reading!

Vanessa

ACKNOWLEDGMENTS

A huge thank you to Stacy Finz at the *San Francisco Chronicle* for making sure that Faith and Siobahn didn't commit any major journalistic gaffs! Any lingering mistakes are entirely my fault. Thanks also to Virna DePaul, Valerie Susan Hayward and Angela Pike for helping make this a better book. Thanks also to Frauke Spanuth of Croco Designs for creating another awesome cover.

Most of all, a continued and heartfelt thank-you to all the readers who have made this series a success!

ABOUT THE AUTHOR

Photo by Gigi Pandian

I confess. I spend way too much time thinking up ways to torture my characters. As a worst-case scenario thinker, I channel my persistently dark what-if questions into writing romantic thrillers that combine intense emotion with action-packed plots.

I'm best known for The Surgical Strike Unit series about a privately run special operations group. My new series, WAR, is set in West Africa, where I lived for a time.

When I'm not writing, listening to music, or playing puzzle games on my mobile device, I help writers learn Scrivener and take long hikes in the nearby hills.

JOIN THE KIERDEVILS

Receive snippets-of-life stories, writing updates, sneak peeks, and other exclusive content such as *The SSU/WAR Bonus Pack* when you join the KierDevils newsletter.

www.vanessakier.com/kierdevils